sinner

Steve L Clark

Orange Octave Press

Sinner

Edited by Don Tackett

Cover art by Matt Wildasin

ISBN 978-1-965316-09-2

ALSO BY

<u>Novellas</u>

The Doors of Chamberlain

Down Home

<u>Short Story Collections</u>

The Collapse of Ordinary

Twisting Parallels

contents

PROLOGUE

I cy wind lashed at her face as Emily Lancaster pushed open the heavy wooden door. The hinges squealed in protest, rusted and stiff from long stretches of time without use and exposure to the elements. With a grunt, she shouldered the door outward a few more inches and slipped through. She turned to close the door behind her out of habit, then remembered her purpose and left it open. She wouldn't be closing any more doors.

At this height, the wind gusts were fierce. Hot tears on her cheeks cooled and frosted over her flushed skin. Despite the frigid blasts of air, she was sweating. A warm heat radiated in her gut. *The demon alcohol.* If only that were all. If her only trespass had been drinking, there would have been hope for forgiveness. She could have confessed her sin and asked God for his grace. If only.

She staggered away from the door and shuffled a few feet to the edge. Ornate layers of bricks formed a waist-high wall around the top of the bell tower. She let the rough edges of brick press into her thighs and wrapped an arm around a support pillar. Her vision swirled, and she closed her eyes. When the dizziness subsided, she opened her eyes and leaned over the wall.

The campus below was beautiful. It was one of the main reasons she had chosen Hallberg Academy. The perfectly manicured lawns and meticulously maintained red brick buildings presented a structured and respectable image. It spoke to her own desire for structure; the need to follow a designed path and live a righteous life. Her parents had been nervous about letting their daughter live on campus. They knew well the temptations of college life. Emily was a good Christian girl, and she had never given them reason to doubt her, but they still feared the wickedness of the world. Emily eventually convinced them in the end, and they gave their blessings.

That was only three months ago. Emily choked back a groan as she stared over the wall at the campus grounds below. They had been right. The devil had seen her coming and ensnared her; all in one night. *Evil needs only one chance to infect the righteous.* That was something her pastor back home used to say. Emily always thought he was dramatic, but now she knew the truth. She had been so naïve; so arrogant in her assumptions. Evil really existed all around them, just waiting for a moment of vulnerability to pounce.

Emily threw back her head and let out a desperate wail of despair. As if in response, the bell tower chimed to life; massive bells swaying back and forth to announce the turn of the hour. Emily clamped her hands over her ears and dropped to her knees. From the top of the tower, the bells were deafening. Her body shook with each vibration.

After the twelfth ring, the bells fell mercifully silent. Emily's head throbbed in pain. With great effort, she gripped the brick wall and pulled herself back to her feet. It was time to do what she'd come here to do. It was all by chance that she had found the door to the tower unlocked.

She hadn't even been sure she could get inside, let alone all the way to the top. That she had found no resistance in her journey confirmed she was making the right decision. This is what God wanted her to do. This is what she deserved. She had thrown everything away in four hours. Four hours ago, she was a young woman living a life of service in the Lord and spreading his teachings to others. She had been tempted several times before and not given in. Like Jesus in the desert, she had remained steadfast in her resolve.

Until tonight. Tonight, despite all the teachings of her life and all the misgivings in her soul, she had opened herself to sin. And sin had climbed all the way in. After months of asking, Emily finally relented and agreed to go to a party with her roommate, Tonya. It started with one drink, and then another. *This isn't so bad,* she had thought. In fact, she found she enjoyed the way her body tingled. Things were funny, and she laughed easier than she ever had before. So she kept going. She had never had a drop of alcohol in her life and now she was on her fifth drink and still going strong.

Then he came.

His name was Paul. She'd never spoken to him before, but he was in one of her classes. He was beautiful. Sometimes Emily would imagine what it would be like to kiss him, then blush in shame and ask forgiveness from the Lord. It was a sin to lust. With her inhibitions buried behind a wall of drink, she had walked straight up to him, wrapped her hand around the back of his head and planted her lips on his. He stiffened in surprise, then returned her kiss with fiery passion. In that moment, Emily's body ignited with feelings unlike anything she had ever felt before. She realized she had spent her entire life in a state of existing rather than truly living. Before she could stop herself, she had asked Paul if he wanted to go somewhere private. When he suggested his dorm room, she had been only too eager. Tonya had tried to stop her, knowing her friend had gone too far, but Emily was oblivious.

What followed was a whirlwind of passion Emily had only fantasized about in her weakest moments. When it was over, she lay in his arms. Like a tidal wave, the blissful ecstasy of their lovemaking crumbled as the reality of what she had just done flooded in. She had gasped and scrambled out of the bed. Paul watched in dazed confusion as she fumbled back into her clothes. He asked if he'd done something wrong, but Emily could not speak. Without a word, she fled from Paul's dorm room and ran down the hall toward the exit. A few boys watched her go, stepping aside to give her room. Emily couldn't force herself to meet their gazes. She knew what they were thinking.

Whore.

She had become one of the most vile of sinners; a direct line from the grotesqueries of Sodom and Gohmorra. Emily knew what God had done to them. There was no hope for her. Not now.

Emily had wandered campus, not consciously aware of where she was going. Upon arriving at the bell tower, she realized God had been leading her all along. She stared up at the structure. There was no fear, only shame and pain. Pain in her heart for failing both her family and herself, but more importantly, for failing her Creator. There was physical pain as well. Her loins throbbed, and she knew she was bleeding. Only the beginning of the pain and torment that would be her punishment. There would be no redemption for her.

My God is a vengeful God.

Now she stood on the edge; both literally and spiritually. Her shoes stuck out over the wall. The top of her head narrowly missed bumping the frame of the tower. Her left hand braced against the support pillar, and she stared at the ground. In the distance, she heard a faint voice.

"Oh, my God! Do you see that? Someone is on the bell tower."

Emily shifted her eyes toward the voice and saw the tiny outline of two people walking along the path approaching the tower.

"Hey! What are you doing? Do you need help?"

There is no help, she thought.

"God forgive me," Emily whispered, knowing her plea fell on deaf ears.

Emily jumped.

The fall took mere seconds, but for a fraction of that time, she wished for God to send an angel to catch her. An angel to stay her hand like he had stopped Abraham from sacrificing his son.

No angel came for her.

Chapter 1

Paul Braxton stared at the email message with glassy eyes. His stubbled chin and jaw rested in one hand, propped on the computer desk. His back and neck were stiff with tension. The message had remained open on his laptop for two days, and he read it countless times.

As many of you know, on the night of December 5th, one of our students climbed to the top of Hering Tower and fell to their death. Police investigations are ongoing. At this time, it is unsure if the incident resulted from an accident or a suicide. Regardless, this is a terrible tragedy, and one we do not take lightly. Hallberg Academy staff and students are family, and we have lost one of our own. Grief counselors are available for anyone who would like to make use of their services. Whether or not this incident was a suicide, we take mental health seriously. We encourage any student or staff member who is struggling to reach out to the health center and seek support.

With deepest sympathy,
Dean Maria Monroe

Paul could recite the message verbatim. Two lines from it echoed loudly in his mind. *At this time, it is unsure if the incident resulted from an accident or a suicide.* Paul felt sure he could answer that question. His mind replayed the memory of her jumping out of his bed and frantically putting her clothes back on. He had seen the horror in her eyes; the regret. He had pleaded for her to stop and tell him what was wrong, but she left him without a word. Her face had spoken volumes in her silence. Even in his own drunken state, he recognized the look in her eyes.

Shame.

The second line from the email that had haunted him for the last two days was the preceding line.

Police investigations are ongoing.

Paul knew it was a matter of time before they came knocking on his door room door. There were lots of people at the party. He could only assume the police were interviewing witnesses. Someone would know Emily had left with him. Frankly, he was amazed they hadn't already arrived. Every sound from the hallway sent a jolt of fear through him. His stomach was a churning ball of guilt, grief, and fear. He had imagined the scenario many times. A pair of detectives would knock at his door. They wore long coats and their faces were stone masks. One would flip open a badge and hold it up for him to see. "Mr. Braxton? We need you to come with us." He would go, and they would put him in an interrogation room. "Eyewitnesses say you were the last person seen with the victim. What can you tell us about the time you spent with Emily Lancaster on the night of December 5th?"

A thunderous knock at the door jolted him from his mental wanderings. His stomach rolled, turning into melting ice collapsing into the void of his bowels. For a moment, he thought he might vomit, and fought back a dry heave.

The knock sounded again, more forcefully this time. "Open up, dude! I forgot my key."

Paul let the words sink in for a moment, and an overwhelming wave of relief washed over him. It wasn't the police. At least, not yet. It was Dex.

Paul lurched out of the computer chair and half-jogged to the door. He pulled it open, and his roommate, Dex, barged past him. Dex slung his backpack onto the bed and flopped down beside it.

"What's your deal, bro?" Dex asked. He pulled the hood of his sweat-shirt up over his crop of disheveled blonde hair. "Are you sick or some-thing? Rebelling? Dropping out? This is day two of you not going to class. What's up?"

Paul shifted his gaze away from Dex and sat back down at the desk. He hadn't told Dex about his night with Emily. Of course, Dex knew what happened to Emily, same as everyone else on campus. Paul had come close the night before to telling him, but backed out at the last minute. Not that he didn't trust Dex. They hadn't known each other before becoming roommates, but Paul had taken to Dex right away. He wasn't worried that Dex would turn him into the police. He also knew he would probably feel a lot better about the situation if he talked to someone and got it off his chest. What held him back was not knowing if Dex would view him as the guilty party he felt himself to be.

"Just not feeling so hot, I guess," Paul said. It wasn't exactly a lie. He felt awful, but it wasn't the flu or anything so mundane. He could feel Dex staring at him from across the room, and turned to face him. Paul saw genuine concern from his friend, and his resolve softened. "Listen, man, can I tell you something in confidence?"

"Absolutely not," Dex said. "I'm recording this conversation and intend to distribute it to all social media platforms as soon as you turn your back."

Paul couldn't help but laugh. "Fuck you, man," he said.

Dex smiled. "What's on your mind, bud?"

"You know that girl that killed herself the other night?"

"Yeah. Everybody does. It's kind of big news."

"Well, I had sex with her." There was a pause as Paul waited for a reaction from Dex. He found he couldn't take his eyes off his shoes.

After a moment, Dex spoke. "So, you're feeling weird because you had sex with a girl who is now dead?" There was a note of confusion in his voice.

"No," Paul said. "I mean, I had sex with her like maybe an hour before she killed herself."

"Oh," Dex replied. "Oh, shit, man. That's, uh, I don't know. That's fucked up. What happened? How did she go from hooking up with you to killing herself? You didn't, uh..." Dex trailed off.

"No," Paul said. "I know what you're thinking, and that's exactly what everyone is going to think. It's what the police are going to think." Paul looked up at Dex and tears shimmered in his eyes. "They're going to think I raped her."

Dex let out a whoosh of air. "Fuck, dude. I don't know what to say. Have you talked to the cops?"

"No, not yet, but I know they will be coming. We left that party at AJ's house together. I'm sure people saw us leave. Honestly, I can't believe they haven't already come for me."

Dex fell into silence for a moment. He propped his chin on both fists and wrinkled his brow. Then he shook his head. "I think you need to go talk to them willingly. Don't wait for them to come to you. If you wait for them to come get you, it's going to look like you were trying to hide. They won't buy you didn't know the girl you slept with was the same girl who jumped off the tower. Get in front of this thing. I'm not saying it will be easy, but you'll feel better if you just get this moving. There had to be more going on. If you didn't force her, then there has to be more to the story. The sooner you talk to them and explain what happened, the sooner you can clear yourself and your conscience."

"I'm afraid, man. What if they don't believe me?"

"I get it, but you have to try. Don't do anything that's going to paint you in a bad light, you know? Definitely don't take off or go home. This sucks, but you're going to have to face it."

Paul sucked in a deep breath, held it, then let it out in a long exhale. It was a breathing technique his mom had taught him when he was young and always helped him get control when he felt like things were too much.

"You're right. I just have to face it head on."

"It's the right call, man. If there's anything I can do to help, say the words. Do you want me to go with you?"

"No, I don't want to involve you anymore than you already are," Paul said as he stood. "I'm going to go to the health center and see if the counselors can't point me to the police. I would imagine they've been told to contact them if anyone gives any information."

"Yeah, that sounds like a plan. It'll be fine."

Paul grabbed the lanyard holding his dorm key and slipped it over his head. "Hopefully, I'll be back later."

"You'll be back, Paul. You did nothing wrong, right? They'll see that."

Paul nodded, but his heart pounded in his chest. He wasn't confident at all. He gave Dex a fist bump and left the room before he could change his mind.

Chapter 2

Tonya Sheffield rubbed her eyes with the back of a trembling fist. The tears had stopped, leaving faded streaks of mascara and puffy eyelids. She cleared her throat and took another sip from the water glass on the table. The two detectives seated across from her waited for her to continue.

"I don't know what else to say. She wouldn't have been at that stupid party if it wasn't for me pushing her to go."

Tonya looked at the detective on the left. He was a tall man, mid-thirties, with dark stubble covering his thin face. His name was Agent Lyons, and Tonya found herself more comfortable speaking directly to him. There was a softness and understanding in his eyes. Compassion. Agent Lyons' partner was much older; a barrel chested man with a shaved head and beady eyes. His badge said Agent Stone, and Tonya found it appropriate. He stared at her with no emotion on his face whatsoever. She felt judged under his gaze.

"I understand how you're feeling," Agent Lyons said. "It's not at all uncommon to feel guilt in a situation like this. But, ultimately, Miss Lancaster was an adult capable of making her own decisions. You encouraged her to go, but whatever happened that led to this tragedy is not your fault. You were a friendly roommate, inviting her to a party with you. I know your intentions were good."

Tonya nodded, then lowered her eyes back to the table.

"The most important thing you can do now is tell us anything you remember that might help shed some light on where she went and what she did after she left the party."

Tonya sighed.

"I know it's hazy for you. But please, walk us through what you remember again."

Hazy. That was an understatement. She barely remembered going back to the dorm room that night. When she woke the next morning to find Emily gone, she wasn't concerned. It was Sunday morning. Emily went to the chapel service on campus every Sunday. She never missed. Tonya was more concerned about the throbbing pain wreaking havoc in her head. She had groaned as she climbed out of bed, still wearing the clothes she'd worn to the party, and staggered out into the hall toward the restrooms. She made it halfway before the swarm of girls approached.

"I can't believe this!"

"Oh my God, Tonya, are you okay?"

"Why would she do that?"

"She was a little weird, but I never imagined this."

Tonya had stared back at the girls in dazed confusion. "What are you talking about?"

"You don't know?"

"Oh, no!"

One girl, a sophomore named Ashley, gave the others a brief glance, then took Tonya by the arm and walked her away from the group. When they were a dozen feet away, she leaned close. "Emily killed herself last night."

Tonya let the words roll around in her brain but could not interpret their meaning. "I don't understand."

"She jumped off the bell tower. She's dead."

"Emily? You mean my Emily? My roommate?"

Ashley nodded.

A flash of memory had then emerged from the fog of her mind; talking Emily into finally going out with her, encouraging her to have a drink and loosen up, cheering as she finished her first beer and grabbed another.

Tonya had staggered away from Ashley. The reality of what she was being told hit her like a truck. Then, without another word, she had run down the hall past the group of girls, into the restroom, and threw up.

"Tonya?"

Agent Stone's voice snapped her from her trance. He stared at her with those cold, emotionless eyes. "Tell us what you remember."

Agent Lyons shifted in his seat, clearly annoyed by his partner's lack of compassion. "Just do the best you can."

"She left with a guy. I think I saw them kissing, but I don't remember for sure. That would have been really out of character for her, but I think it happened. I think I tried to catch up to her, but I couldn't get through the crowd before they left. When I got outside, they were gone."

"You think you tried?" Agent Stone asked.

Tonya felt heat swarm over her face, and the words left her mouth before she could stop herself. "I don't fucking remember! I was drunk, okay?"

Agent Stone peered at her. He clenched his jaw, but said nothing. He scribbled something in his notepad, then returned to staring.

"Come on, Tom," Agent Lyons said. "Give her a break."

Agent Stone shrugged his shoulders.

"It's okay, Tonya. You're not in trouble. We're just trying to figure this out. That's all."

"I know." She propped her elbows on the table and clasped her head with both hands. Slowly drawing in a deep breath, she closed her eyes and focused on her compromised memory of the party.

Emily is on her fourth or fifth drink. Tonya had been counting, aware and cautious that her roommate had never drank alcohol, but her own drinks made it difficult. After all, she wasn't a babysitter. And Emily was having a good time. Tonya had never seen her so relaxed and outgoing. Her laugh was contagious, and she had a beautiful smile - both things Tonya had only glimpsed in very rare occurrences. The girl was always so serious. It was refreshing to see her having a good time for once. Then the boy came.

When Emily saw him, her entire demeanor changed. Her alcohol fueled goofiness shifted. She wasn't laughing anymore, though a sly smile teased her lips. Again, it was an expression Tonya had never seen from Emily. It was an intense look, passionate and primal. It reminded Tonya of how a hungry animal reacts when it has spotted potential prey.

Tonya didn't recognize the boy, so she asked Emily who he was. "Who is that handsome fella you've got your eyes on?"

Emily gave her a name, but it was lost in the void of alcohol forgetfulness. Someone from one of her classes. Was it psychology? She couldn't remember.

Then Emily was on the move. With a bold confidence Tonya could never have imagined, she watched in awe as Emily marched across the crowded room, slid a hand behind his head, and planted her lips on his. The boy had stiffened in surprise, but quickly recovered. When the kiss was over, Tonya watched the pair talk animatedly. She hadn't wanted to interfere, so she watched from a distance. This was dangerous territory, and Tonya knew it. Even then, a sense of dread had crept in - a twisting knot in her already distressed stomach.

After several minutes of watching them talk, Tonya relaxed a bit and rejoined the surrounding conversations. It was not until right before Emily and the boy passed through the front door and outside that Tonya realized they were gone. She had gone after them, that nervous dread now amplified tenfold, but by the time she had shouldered her way through the crowd and stumbled out onto the lawn, she had lost them. Pockets of people surrounding a pair of beer pong tables cluttered her view.

Emily was gone.

"Tonya?"

Tonya lifted her head and opened her eyes. Agent Lyons looked expectantly at her. Agent Stone stared at the table with a frown on his face.

"Do you remember anything?"

"She left with a guy. I don't know his name. He's not someone I knew. She said he was in one of her classes. I tried to catch her when I saw them leaving together, but I couldn't get to her fast enough. They were gone by the time I got outside. That's all I remember."

Agent Lyons reached across the table and gave her hand a reassuring squeeze. "That's very helpful. If the guy she left with was in a class with her, that narrows down our search drastically."

"Would you recognize him if you saw him again?" Agent Stone asked. This bit of information seemed to have energized the stoic man, and his face no longer showed the annoyance he previously exhibited.

"I think so. Yeah."

"Good. We'll likely be calling on you to do that. It's a fair bet that whoever he was, this guy won't admit he was the last person seen with her."

Tonya frowned. "Do you think it might not have been a suicide? Do you think this guy might have done this?"

"Well," Agent Stone replied, "the eyewitnesses at the scene only saw her on the tower. We don't know for sure if anyone was up there with her. It's possible there could have been, and they got away without being seen. We have to look at all possibilities. It's an open investigation."

Agent Lyons pulled a card from his breast pocket and slid it across the table. "If you think of anything else, call me. Day or night. We will be in touch as well if we have any follow-up questions. Thank you, Tonya. This is a difficult situation. We appreciate your help."

Tonya replied with a tight-lipped smile. "Am I free to go?"

"Of course."

The detectives stood, and Agent Lyons held the door for her. "We'll be in touch."

She nodded and left the small office, glancing at her watch. Her next class started in fifteen minutes. She could probably make it if she hurried, but quickly acknowledged she wasn't going. Her mind was racing, and it would be a complete waste of time to sit through an hour of calculus. There was no way she had the mental capacity to be productive after the interview. She was exhausted; mentally, physically, and emotionally. At this moment, the only place she wanted to be was in her bed. Sleep wouldn't make it all go away, but it would let her shut it off for a few blissful hours.

Tonya made for the double doors leading out of the building toward the quad. Light rain sprinkled the pavement, and she pulled the small umbrella from her bag. As she pressed the button and opened it up, she collided with someone walking up the short flight of stone steps.

"Oh, I'm sorry..."

Her eyes widened as she locked eyes with the man she had bumped into.

It was him.

CHAPTER 3

Agent Elliot Lyons watched the young lady make her way out of the office, then closed the door behind her. He sighed as he turned back to his partner. Tom Stone stared at him thoughtfully.

"Interesting," Tom said.

Elliot chewed at his bottom lip and nodded. He returned to his seat and flipped the page of his notebook. "Definitely something to this."

"You thinking what I'm thinking?" Tom asked.

"Depends what you're thinking. If you think this mystery guy was up there with her and shoved her off the bell tower, then no. I don't buy that he could get back down and disappear with no one seeing him."

"It was late. There weren't many people around."

"I know, but the eyewitness screamed when our girl jumped. Lot of commotion drawing attention. Police response was fast, and they reported multiple people at the scene when they arrived."

"Guy could have blended in with the crowd. Some sick fuck wanting to get a good look at his damage."

Elliot considered for a moment, then shook his head. "I just don't think so."

"I don't either, really. Just playing devil's advocate. I think she jumped. Question is why? Medical records on file with the school don't show any history of mental illness."

"Doesn't mean she didn't have it. Depression and anxiety are silent killers."

"I know that," Tom said. He glanced at his watch. "The parents are due to arrive in about three hours. That might help determine if they were aware of any mood disorders."

Elliot skimmed through his notes. "The school year started two months ago. Emily Lancaster and Tonya Sheffield moved into the dorm together a week prior to the start of classes. No warning signs of depression noted from Tonya."

"Right," Tom replied, "which leads me to agree with the roommate's suspicion about this guy she left with. Quiet girl who doesn't do the party scene gets drunk and leaves with a boy, then kills herself shortly after? That, my friend, is a lead."

Elliot nodded. "We need to pull Emily's class schedule and class lists from each of her courses. If this guy is responsible, he's likely to run."

"Maybe. Maybe not. Some of these kids have had silver spoons shoved up their asses for so long they think they're untouchable."

"That's a stereotype," Elliot said.

"One with a substantial amount of truth behind it, in my experience. I've been doing this a long time, and I don't have enough fingers and toes to count how many times some privileged little brat came strutting into an interrogation room with a high-priced lawyer on a leash. Think mommy and daddy's money will buy them out of anything."

Elliot shrugged, conceding to Tom's point.

"While you work on pulling the class schedules, I'm going to track down this cat who threw the party." Tom checked his notes. "AJ Beaumont. Jesus, I can already tell this kid's gonna be a treat."

Elliot chuckled. "You're doing it again."

"Wait and see if I'm wrong."

"Administration should have his address," Elliot said.

Tom pushed his chair back and stood. "I'll meet you back here after I question the party host. We'll get prepared for the parents." He paused, shoving his hands in the pockets of his gray trousers. "I won't lie to you, Elliot. It's going to be rough."

Elliot looked up, raising an eyebrow.

"I know you haven't been involved in a case like this before. It's tough asking parents questions about their child who has just died. Doesn't matter if it's murder, suicide, accidental, or any other way to go. These folks just lost a child."

"I understand."

"I know you think you do. On an intellectual level, you're right." Tom leaned over and planted his knuckles on the table. "But you don't have kids. There's only so much you can learn from books and training. Until you have a child, and you find out just how much of your heart and soul got taken from you to make them, you don't really understand."

Elliot leaned back. "I get you."

"Good. If they were to show up early, and I'm not back yet, don't start without me. I don't want you dealing with that on your own."

"Sure."

Elliot watched Tom go, closing the door behind him. He closed his eyes and let silence fill the room. He didn't like where this was headed. Despite his caution to Tom about stereotyping, his suspicions were leading him down a similar path. The quick assumption to make was the boy she left the party with had raped Emily. The coroner's report would be available soon, and that would shed light on whether or not there was evidence of sexual assault. What else would push Emily to make such a drastic choice?

Too many loose ends, he thought. *Don't make assumptions. Let the evidence lead the way.*

At that, he pulled his phone from his pocket and dialed a number from the printed directory the university staff had given him. The line picked up after one ring.

"Administration office, this is Nancy. How may I assist you?"

"Hi Nancy. This is Detective Elliot Lyons."

"Oh, hello detective." The cheerful pitch of her voice softened. "What can I do for you?"

"I need a list of all the classes Miss Lancaster was taking, as well as a list of all the students enrolled in each of those classes."

"Of course, sir. Is there an email address you'd like me to use?"

Elliot gave her the address, thanked her, and hung up the phone.

Why did you do it? He pondered while he waited for the email. *Why did you do it?*

Agent Tom Stone hurried through the lobby of the health center and stepped outside. The overcast sky had given way, and a steady drizzle of cool October rain dotted the sidewalks. With his head down, he retrieved his phone and called the administration office. A pocket of students hustled past him toward the building, eager to get inside before the rain picked up. Growling thunder rang out, and he pressed his finger to his ear to better hear the admin secretary. A young man and a woman holding an umbrella stood nearby, staring at him as he passed, but he paid them no mind. Tom figured they recognized him as a detective. Morbid curiosity in times of tragedy got the better of most people.

The nondescript Chevy Impala he was driving sat parked half a block down the narrow street. He jogged the remaining thirty yards while he waited for the secretary to give him the address and slid smoothly into the car. Her voice came back on the line, and he scribbled down the address for one Andrew Jackson Beaumont.

Jesus Christ, he thought. *I knew this kid was gonna be trouble. With a name like that, how could he not?*

Tom thanked her for the information and hung up. He glanced at the dashboard clock. Almost two in the afternoon. The parents were due to arrive around five, and he was determined not to let Elliot deal with them on his own. He would have to be quick with this kid; get the information he needed and get out. Tom hoped like hell the kid would cooperate without being a pompous asshole.

You're stereotyping again. Elliot's words echoed in his mind, and he smirked. He knew the kid was right, but he also knew his own intuition had served him well. More times than he could count. A big part of being a successful detective was having solid instincts and trusting your gut.

His gut told him there was more to this story than just a suicide. Something else was going on here. He could feel it in his bones. *Trust your instincts and follow the leads.*

Tom started the car, punched 118 Linden Avenue into the GPS, checked the side mirror for traffic, and pulled away. The windshield wipers whisked back and forth as the rain picked up. He reached the stop sign, then turned left; taking him away from campus and toward the small residential area that served as off-campus housing. In his rear-view mirror, he could see the bell tower standing majestically in the distance. As if on queue, the bells clanged to life, jingling a melody to sound the turn of the hour. In his mind, he imagined the poor girl plummeting from the top railing to her death. He thought of the parents on their way to identify their daughter's body and collect her belongings.

Sometimes he hated this job.

CHAPTER 4

Paul froze at the top of the stairs. He'd been lost in his thoughts; the dread of the coming confrontation with the police left him nauseous. He'd kept his eyes planted on the concrete stairs in front of him lest the looming facade of the health center and questions awaiting inside send him running back the way he'd come. The jarring collision with the girl was startling enough, but her expression afterward sent needles of ice through his veins. It was a look of astonished recognition.

She knew.

Or, at least, his mind told him so. He scanned his memory, but could not place the girl, though she seemed vaguely familiar. There was no doubt, however, that she recognized him.

"It's you," she said.

Those two words felt like a sledgehammer blow to his chest. A wave of dizziness washed over him, and his cheeks warmed.

"I'm sorry?" Paul asked, cringing at the faux ignorance.

"You're the guy she left with."

Paul searched his mind for the right thing to say. His mouth moved, desperately trying to form words, but what came out was a choke. His eyes welled and shame washed over him. "I didn't do...what you think I did."

The girl stared at him apprehensively.

"I swear. That's why I'm here. I came to talk to the police. We left together, and we slept together, but I swear I didn't rape her." Paul sighed and dropped his head back on his shoulders, letting the rain hit his face. "When it was over, she kind of freaked out and left without telling me why. I swear on my life, I didn't rape her. She was all over me. I don't know why she did what she did, but I swear I didn't force her to do anything."

He dropped his head, unable to make eye contact with the girl. The roar of his heart pounding in his chest was all he could hear while he waited for her to respond. The silence held for agonizing seconds. A man in a dark suit rushed past them, and from his peripheral, he saw the girl stiffen as she watched the man go. Paul turned to see. The man was rushing through the rain down the street. Paul could tell from the way he carried himself that he was a cop.

"That's the detective," the girl said.

Paul turned toward her and was relieved to see the suspicion had gone from her face.

"I just told them about you. Well, kind of. I don't know your name and I didn't give a description, because I couldn't really remember. I thought I'd know you if you saw you, but I didn't think it would be as soon as I walked outside."

"I'm Paul."

"Yeah, that sounds right. She told me your name, but I couldn't remember it. Paul."

Paul shook his head. "She told you about me?"

"At the party, yeah. I'm Tonya. I'm her roommate...*was* her roommate."

"I just had one class with her. Didn't even know her name until she came up to me at the party. She walked right up to me and kissed me. I had never even spoken to her before."

The rain picked up, turning from soft taps on the earth to a steadily growing roar. Paul motioned for Tonya to follow him to the edge of the building, where a balcony supported by large stone pillars provided cover.

"So, what did you tell them about me?"

"Not much. Like I said, I didn't know who you were. I told them what Emily said about you and how she went up and kissed you like that, and then-"

"You told them she walked up and kissed me first? Good. I'm glad you saw that. It makes me sound like a jerk, but I'm scared to death here. I need them to understand that I didn't start any of this. She was all over me. I didn't take advantage of her. I need them to believe that."

Tonya peered at him. He could see her processing his words. He was desperate for her to believe him. "I don't know why she did what she did, but I swear I did nothing to hurt her."

"I believe you," Tonya said. "I'm more responsible for what happened than you are."

"What do you mean?"

"She wouldn't have been at the party if I hadn't pushed her to do it; wouldn't have been there, wouldn't have been drunk, wouldn't have left with you. She wasn't a party girl, but I kept pushing her to go have some fun. None of this would have happened if I would have left her alone."

Paul didn't know what to say at first. He'd been so consumed with his own guilt and fears that he hadn't considered what Tonya was feeling.

He assumed she would fall in line with what he expected; suspicion that this was his fault. Instead, in contrast to his fear of being judged responsible, Tonya felt solely responsible for Emily's fate. Though they approached from different angles, they stood together under the weight of uncertainty.

"Damn," he said, finally breaking the silence. "I understand what you're saying, but you can't pin it all on yourself. I mean, we're all adults here. You didn't hold her at gunpoint."

"I know, but it doesn't make it any easier."

"I guess not."

There was another awkward silence. Paul wanted to reassure her, but he knew from his own feelings that peace would not be coming soon. It would take time.

"So, are you still talking to the cops?"

"I think I have to. They'll be looking for me, so it's a better look if I come to them first, right?"

"Yeah, I think so. Do you want me to go in with you?"

The offer surprised Paul. It touched him she would offer. In only a few brief minutes, they had established a kinship; two people united under a shared trauma. "Thank you, but I don't want to cause you any more trouble. Plus, it might seem strange if you go back in there with the guy who you just told them you didn't know."

"That's true," Tonya said. "Well, good luck. Just tell them the truth. For what it's worth, I believe you, and if telling them that makes a difference, I will."

A lump formed in Paul's throat, and his face flushed. He never considered himself a very emotional guy, but the last day had changed him. Her belief meant everything to him. If she believed, then maybe the police would, too?

"Thank you, Tonya. Genuinely, thank you." He shifted and took a step away, then stopped, feeling awkward. "How can I get in touch with you? I mean, like, if I need you to back me up on what happened at the party? Or if you need someone to talk to?"

"Yeah, sure," Tonya replied. She reached into the small cross-body purse she wore and fished out a pen and a receipt. She scribbled her number on the back and handed it to him. "They have my number, too," she said, nodding toward the building. "I'm sure they'll call me if they want to ask follow-up questions."

"Right," Paul said. He felt dumb. He didn't want her to think he was using this situation to pick up on her and get her number. The potential threat looming had made him feel defensive about his motives for everything. He desperately needed a friend right now, someone who understood what he was going through. Tonya felt like the closest thing he was going to find.

She must have sensed his discomfort. "But call me anyway, later. I want to know how it goes when you talk to them."

Paul felt a wave of relief. "I will. Thank you."

They held each other's gaze for a moment, then Paul turned, sucked in a lungful of air, and made for the front door of the health center. It was time to face this head-on. He pulled open the door and stepped inside, while a growl of thunder sounded from above.

CHAPTER 5

AJ Beaumont held the small pipe to his lips, rolled his thumb over the lighter, lowered the flame into the bowl, and sucked the smoke into his lungs. The crackling of burning herb was barely audible over the drone of the Bluetooth speaker. He had the bass boost maxed, and the Spotify mix of nineties grunge made the speaker vibrate noisily on the computer desk. He leaned back in the desk chair, held his breath with closed eyes, then erupted into a coughing fit.

Gotta cough to get off, he thought to himself, then chuckled. His eyes watered, and he could already feel them puffing and glazing over.

Good shit.

He readied the lighter to take another hit when the doorbell rang. The sudden chime startled him and he dropped the pipe. Charred weed and ash scattered across the carpet.

"Fuck me!"

A sharp pounding sounded from the front of the house; three hard knocks.

"Who the fuck?" AJ stood and peaked out the bedroom window. It faced the street, and he saw a gray car parked at the curb. It wasn't a car he recognized, but that wasn't that strange. He couldn't know what all his people drove, and his house was a popular stop. AJ had a reputation for being the guy to go to when you needed some party favors. He preferred people give him a heads up before they stopped by, but it didn't always work out that way.

Still annoyed about spilling his weed, he stomped out of the bedroom and toward the front door. The heavy knocking came again, immediately followed by another chime from the doorbell.

"I'm coming, motherfucker!"

He grabbed the doorknob, slung it open, and froze.

The man standing outside was not a college student, and AJ was pretty damn sure he wasn't here to buy dope. This guy had cop written all over him; stocky, shaved head, dark suit, and no emotion in his face whatsoever.

"Are you Andrew Jackson Beaumont?"

Fuck.

"Who's asking?"

"Detective Tom Stone." The man pulled a folded wallet from inside his jacket and flipped it open, showing his badge.

AJ stiffened, not failing to notice the gun holstered to his hip when the jacket lifted as he returned the wallet to his pocket.

Someone fucking ratted me out.

"I'm AJ. What can I do for you, officer?"

"It's detective," the man said. His voice was icy.

"Sorry, *Detective Stone.* What can I do for you?" AJ immediately regretted the sarcasm, but he couldn't take it back. He thought he saw the ghost of a smile twitch at the corner of the detective's mouth.

"Did you have a party here Saturday night?"

"I had some friends over, sure."

The detective reached back into his jacket, this time producing a 3x5 photograph. "Do you remember this girl being at the party?"

AJ glanced at the picture and shrugged. He hadn't known the girl then, but he definitely knew her now. She was the girl who took a dive off the tower.

"There were a lot of girls here. I don't remember everyone. She might have been."

"Think a little harder, Mr. Beaumont." Detective Stone's icy glare burned.

AJ shifted uncomfortably. "Sure, man. She was probably here. If you're here asking me, then I assume someone already told you she was. I don't remember seeing her myself, but it's a big house. Lot of people spread around. Totally possible she was here, and I didn't know."

Detective Stone studied AJ. "You are correct. We have a witness stating she was here, and then left with someone. I am hoping you could help us identify the man she left with."

"Sorry, can't help you."

"Mr. Beaumont, are you aware of what happened to this girl?"

"Yeah, I think everyone around here does. Not everyday someone jumps off the tower."

"No, it is not. I would very much like to understand how and why it happened - and only a short time after she left your party."

AJ bristled. "Look, man, I don't know what to tell you. If you were told she was here, then she probably was. I don't know who she came with, who she left with, or why she painted the sidewalk with her..."

Detective Stone moved with unexpected quickness, planting his fore-arm against AJ's chest and pinning him against the door frame. AJ yelped in pain as the back of his head thudded off the wood.

"You listen to me, you arrogant little shit. That was someone's daughter. Something caused her to do what she did, and it's a goddamn tragedy. Show some fucking respect."

"This is police brutality, man," AJ spat. "You can't put your hands on me. My dad is an attorney, and he'll have your job when he finds out what you did."

"I don't care if your dad is Jesus fucking Christ. You can call him and cry as soon as we're done here. While we wait, I'll search the premises. From the smell of you, I feel very confident I'm going to find a few things you wouldn't want a cop to find."

"You can't search my house without a warrant. I'm not stupid."

"Why do I care about a warrant? Your daddy's going to have my job, remember?"

AJ fell silent, grimacing as the detective leaned in and pushed harder against his collarbone.

"Or we can be civilized men." At that, Detective Stone released him and stepped back onto the porch. His face was beet red, and AJ could see his jaw clenching and grinding through his cheeks. "Now, I'll ask you one more time. Can you give me any information that would help us track down the guy she left with? I believe you didn't see her, but I don't believe there weren't other people here you could reach out to that might know who it was."

AJ stared back at the detective. His hands shook; anger and fear forced adrenaline through his body. He wanted to tell him to get the fuck off his porch, but he knew better. He had played the *my dad is an attorney* card a few times before, and it had always worked. Something about Detective Stone made him feel like the guy wasn't bluffing.

"I can make a few calls, see if anybody knows."

"That would be wonderful, Mr. Beaumont." Detective Stone pulled a card from his pocket and handed it to AJ. "Make your calls, and if you get any information that can help us, you call me."

AJ took the card without looking at it and shoved it in the pocket of his baggy gym shorts. "Yes, sir."

Detective Stone smiled. "Yes, sir. I like that. You're learning already."

AJ's face burned red.

"I appreciate your time and cooperation, Mr. Beaumont. I'll be in touch."

AJ said nothing as the detective strolled casually back down the sidewalk to the street and back to his car. He stood still in the doorway until the red taillights disappeared around the corner.

"Mother fucker," AJ muttered, then slammed the door.

Tom Stone turned off Linden Avenue. His mouth twisted in a tight grimace.

He fucked up.

He let that cocky shithead get under his skin. It wasn't the first time he'd lost his cool, but it had been a long time. He was well aware of his hot temper; as his employment record would concur. He'd done a lot of work to get it under control. At first it was mandated anger management counseling, but he'd kept it going even after completing his required hours. He got a lot out of therapy. It had served him well.

Until now.

What bothered him most about it was the kid hadn't really said anything to warrant such a hostile reaction. Sure, he had made a disrespectful comment, but that wasn't unusual for guys like him. Tom had heard much worse. Something about this case had his emotions stirred up higher.

You know what that something is. As much as he tried to ignore it or downplay it, he knew why.

His own daughter, Shannon, was the same age as Emily. Unlike Emily, there most definitely was a history of depression and mental illness. Shannon had tried to take her own life. More than once. She'd come damn close. It had been divine intervention that Tom had arrived at just the right time to call the paramedics and save her. Divine intervention or blind luck. Tom preferred to lean toward intervention.

Luck runs out.

Things seemed to be better now with Shannon. After trying out a few different therapists, they had finally found one that was making a difference. Shannon still had her bad days, but there was a hope there Tom hadn't seen in her for a very long time. It gave him a sense of hope for the future, but the fear of a relapse always hung heavy on his heart; a black cloud hanging on the horizon.

This case struck too close to home for him. Maybe it was time to consider a change of departments? Or hell, maybe even early retirement? He was fifty-five years old. Was it too late to change career tracks? He didn't think it was, but he also didn't like the idea of milking his last few years. He enjoyed being a detective. When bad things happen, people need answers. He liked being in the business of providing those answers.

Tom thought again of AJ. His gut feeling was the kid would keep quiet and play ball. If he wasn't able to come up with any leads, Tom would not push the issue. He'd pushed enough.

His phone rang, and he picked it up and eyed the caller ID. He wasn't expecting a call back so fast from the kid, but maybe he'd scared him more than he thought? The name on the screen said Elliot Lyons. Tom slid his thumb to answer the call and tapped the speaker icon.

"What's up, Elliot?"

"Guess who just stopped in to see us?"

"It's not the parents, is it?" Tom asked.

"No. It's our mystery man who left the party with Emily. Here of his own free will."

"Well, how about that? I'm on my way back. Let him sit until I get there."

"I wouldn't dream of starting without you."

"See, kid?" Tom said. "Sometimes this job is easy. Don't get used to it, but now and then, your suspects come to you."

"Yeah, well, we'll see. I'm not jumping to conclusions."

"Good," Tom said, and hung up the phone. He pressed a little harder on the gas pedal and picked up speed. The bell tower crept closer in the distance.

Well, how about that?

CHAPTER 6

Paul watched the detective through the open office door. He had stepped far enough away that Paul couldn't hear what he was saying. His knee bounced under the desk while he waited for the detective to return. After a moment, Paul saw him end the call and turn back toward the office. The detective walked casually back and leaned inside, gripping each side of the doorframe.

"My partner is on his way back. Should only be a few minutes, and then we can get started. Would you like some water while we wait?"

Paul shook his head. "No, thank you."

"Okay. I've got another call to make, if you'll excuse me?"

"Sure."

Paul slumped back into the chair after the detective left. This time, he walked further away and out of sight. He had introduced himself as Detective Lyons. He seemed friendly enough. When Paul told him who he was, and why he was there, he had expected to see judgment and suspicion on the man's face. He was relieved to find that was not his reaction at all. He had looked a bit surprised, but had covered it up well. Intrigued was the word that came to Paul's mind. It gave him hope that maybe his coming willingly would indeed help his case. His stomach was still a churning ball of nerves. It felt like a hive of bees was swarming in his gut, and his heartbeat thudded in his chest. His anxiety was still at panic levels, but not feeling like the detective had immediately found him guilty took a bit of the edge off.

While he waited for Detective Lyons to return, he ran through the events of the night in his mind. It was incredibly important he kept his story straight and told them everything. He was without a doubt their number one suspect at the moment, and he knew if his story changed at all or he left anything out, it could come with dire consequences.

His eyes were closed in concentration when a voice jolted him.

"Good afternoon. Mr. Braxton, is it?"

Paul looked up quickly. Detective Lyons was in the doorway, but another man had walked in ahead of him. His voice was devoid of any pleasantness, and he stared at Paul with a stony gaze. Paul swallowed hard, fighting a surge of nausea. "Yes, sir. Paul Braxton."

"Paul Braxton, my name is Detective Stone. You've met my partner, Detective Lyons. He tells me you have information regarding Emily Lancaster?"

Detective Lyons closed the office door, and both men took their seats across the desk. The room suddenly felt tiny, as if the walls were closing in. Paul felt his breathing intensify. *I'm about to have a panic attack,* he thought.

Detective Lyons picked up on it immediately. "Everything is fine, Paul. We're just talking. If you have information that can help us figure out what happened here, we want to hear it."

Paul cursed himself silently. He was making himself look guiltier by the second. *Get your shit together and tell them the truth.* He took a long inhale, then slowly let it out.

"I was with Emily the night she...did what she did."

"You were with her on the tower?" Detective Stone asked.

"No, before that. We were at the same party, and we left together."

"Were you two friends?" Detective Lyons asked.

"No. We actually had never really met before the party. We had psychology together, but we'd never spoken."

Detective Lyons wrote a note, then continued. "What happened at the party? How were you introduced?"

"I had just gotten there, and she came up to me out of the blue and kissed me. It was very unexpected. Like I said, I didn't really even know her. After that, we talked for a while and she asked me if I wanted to leave the party."

"Did you leave then?" Stone asked.

"Yes."

"Where did you go?"

"We went back to my dorm room. She said she wanted to go somewhere private."

"How would you describe Emily's actions during this time? You said she kissed you. Rather unusual to be kissed by someone you've never met," Detective Lyons said.

"She had definitely been drinking," Paul said. He flinched as he said it, knowing how it sounded, but he was determined to tell everything.

"Had you been drinking as well?" Stone asked.

"Yes, a little. I had a few beers."

"How many is a few?"

"Three or four. I don't know how many she had had before I got there, but she only had one while we were together at the party. She was very flirty. It was pretty clear what she was thinking when she asked me to leave with her."

"And what was that?" Stone asked.

Paul closed his eyes. This was not going how he wanted it to go. "She wanted to have sex. Listen, I know how it sounds, and I know what you're thinking. It's why I was afraid to come to you, at first. I swear to God I didn't rape her. We went back to my room, and she was all over me. She was definitely in the driver's seat. This wasn't a regular weekend kind of thing for me. It was all very unexpected. But I swear on my life that I didn't force her to do anything."

"It's okay, Paul," Detective Lyons said. "We're not accusing you of anything. We're just getting the facts. What happened after you had sex with Miss Lancaster?"

"She freaked out. Everything had been fine, and then she jumped out of bed and put her clothes back on. She didn't say anything. I couldn't get her to answer me. I asked her if I did something wrong, and if she was okay, but she wouldn't talk. She had this crazy look on her face, like she had seen something terrible. Then she ran out of the room. I didn't see her again after that."

There was a moment of silence. Both detectives watched Paul. He felt like they were waiting for him to slip out of character. He was on a tightrope without a net, and they were waiting for him to fall.

"Did you try to go after her?" Detective Lyons asked.

"No. I wanted to, but I thought that might make it worse. She already wasn't talking to me, and she was so freaked out, I thought it was a bad idea. I didn't want to scare her."

"Do you think she was afraid of you?" Detective Stone asked.

"I don't know. She didn't look scared, really. More like something disgusted or horrified her. I don't know how to explain it. It was like a flick of a switch. One minute we're laying in bed together, and the next she's running like she's seen a ghost or something awful. I don't know."

Paul dropped his head in his hands and sobbed. The weight of guilt, fear, and anxiety had finally broken him. "I don't know why she did it. I feel like it's my fault, but I don't know why. We didn't do anything she didn't want to do. I swear to God, I didn't hurt her."

Paul sat hunched over, shoulders rocking. The detectives remained quiet and let him get through it. When he regained control of himself, he sat back and wiped his eyes with the back of his hand. "So, what now?"

The detectives stared back at him in silence. Detective Lyons turned to his partner. Stone gave a curt nod but said nothing.

"I think that's enough for now," Detective Lyons said. "Would you mind giving us a contact number for you in case we have follow-up questions?"

Paul was baffled. He expected there to be more questions or even the possibility of them placing him under arrest. That was an exaggerated thought, but it didn't feel any less like a realistic outcome to him. "Yes, of course." He gave the detectives his number and rose shakily to his feet. "So, I'm free to go?"

"You seem surprised by that, Mr. Braxton," Detective Stone said. He was studying Paul with those blank, unsettling eyes. "Is there anything else you want to tell us? Something that might change our minds? From what you've told us, you've done nothing inappropriate. Nothing illegal. Why wouldn't you be free to go?"

Paul's face flushed with embarrassment. He'd told the truth of the story, so no reason to stop now. "Honestly, I didn't think you would believe me. I am well aware of how this looks. It's your job to investigate crimes. Under these circumstances, I realize I'm the most likely person to have done something wrong. All I could do was tell the truth, and I did. Every word."

"That's all we ask of you, Paul." Detective Lyons stood and escorted Paul to the door. "This is a tragic situation, and I understand you're under a lot of stress, given your relationship with Emily. You did the right thing by coming to us. It speaks to your character. Go get some rest and we'll be in touch if we have more questions."

Paul nodded. The sympathy shown by Detective Lyons was a massive relief. He glanced at Detective Stone, who still sat in his chair. Stone held his gaze. His face was unreadable.

"Thank you," Paul said. He left the office and made for the exit, not turning back when he heard the office door closing behind him. *Never look a gift horse in the mouth.* That was something his grandfather used to say. This had gone better than he had hoped. He wasn't entirely sure they believed him, but they seemed open to the possibility of believing him. That was all he could ask for.

Paul stepped outside and found the rain had stopped. The downpour had brought cooler temperatures with it, and he relished the chilled breeze on his flushed skin. For the first time since he saw the news about Emily, he thought things might work out okay.

CHAPTER 7

Tonya woke to a knock at the door. She pushed herself upright and squinted around the room. It was still daylight, but the overcast sky disguised the time. She remembered coming back to her room after talking with the detectives and laying down on the bed, but she hadn't meant to fall asleep.

The knock came again, a bit more forcefully this time.

"Coming." She stood, ran fingers through her hair to tame her bed head, and opened the door.

A man and woman stood outside in the hall. They were middle-aged and strikingly old-fashioned. The man wore black dress pants and a navy blue button-up shirt. He was clean shaven and neatly groomed, with his hair parted and combed to the side. His jaw clenched, and he looked at her with beady eyes. The woman wore an ankle length, flower-printed dress with long sleeves and a high collar. Her hair was pulled up in a tight bun. She wore no makeup, and her mouth twisted into a miserable frown. Her eyes were bloodshot, with puffy dark bags underneath them.

Tonya stared at them in confusion. Her sleep fogged mind was not prepared to process the couple knocking at her door. "Can I help you?"

"We're here for her things," the man said.

All at once, she understood, and her heart broke. These were Emily's parents.

"Of course, I'm so sorry. Please, come in. I didn't know you would come today." She stepped aside and let the couple into the room. "I can't tell you how sorry I am for your loss."

The man turned toward her. "Not as sorry as I am, I'm quite sure. "

Tonya said nothing, sending her eyes to the wood flooring. She was ashamed to stand in the same room as them, knowing the despair they must be feeling, all while she harbored so much guilt.

"We raised her right; to love God in all His glory and fear Him in all his wrath," the man said.

"Heathen," hissed Emily's mother. Her voice was pinched with anger.

"She has brought shame upon our family. Suicide is a tremendous sin. It is not the right of us to take life, for only He knows when it is time to be called home."

"A fallen angel, cast into the abyss." Spittle flew from the small woman's lips. Her face twisted in an ugly rage.

Tonya's lip trembled. She was not a religious person, but she recognized that they too felt responsible for Emily's death; as if they had failed as parents. "You raised a wonderful daughter," she said with a quivering voice. "I feel just as responsible. If only I hadn't talked her into going to that party, none of this would have happened." A sob burst from her throat and she dropped her head again. Fat tears dripped from her cheeks and floated to the floor. She felt hands on her shoulders and sagged. How could she stand here and take comfort from Emily's parents after what had happened?

The grip on her shoulders tightened. Fingers dug deep into the muscle and shocks of pain radiated down her arms. Tonya jerked her head up in surprise. Emily's father's red face was inches from hers. He snorted through his nose.

"A party? You took our precious girl, our servant of God, to a den of debauchery and filth?"

Emily's mother wailed in despair, then fixed wild eyes on Tonya. "A temptress! Like Lucifer in the desert tempting Jesus for forty days. You defiled our daughter and fed her to the beast."

"It is no wonder, then," the man said. He squeezed even harder, causing Tonya to yelp, then shook her violently. "You let the devil in her and the devil had his way. And now she will sit beside his throne in the pits of Hell for all eternity!"

Tonya struggled to break loose, but his grip only tightened. "Someone, help me! Please!"

Suddenly, Emily's mother's hand streaked across her face. Tonya heard the impact a split second before the pain registered. A hot, tingling sensation rippled across her jaw.

"There is no help for the likes of you. A servant of the dark one. A corrupter of innocence," screamed the man.

"Oh, my God!"

All three of them turned in surprise to the door, which still stood open. A small group of girls stood gaping into the room.

"Let her go!"

Two of them rushed into the room and pushed Emily's father. He slung Tonya backwards, finally releasing the grip on her arms.

"I'm calling the police," said the other in the hall.

Emily's parents stepped past the girls and returned to the hallway. Her mother hissed at them like a feral cat as they went.

Tonya watched them turn down the hall and disappear from view, then burst into hysterical tears. The two girls who had pushed the man away dropped beside her, both wrapping their arms around her in a tight embrace.

Tonya closed her eyes and wept.

"Do you believe him?"

Elliot Lyons sat leaned back in his chair with his legs outstretched in front of him and fingers laced behind his head. "I do. Or, at least, I have no reason not to believe him with our current information."

Tom contemplated him, then nodded. "I'm with you. The kid was a nervous wreck, but he didn't strike me as the nervous someone gets when they are trying to get away with something. He didn't contradict any of the eyewitness reports we've gathered so far or that he had sex with her. My gut says he's on the level."

"I agree. He seemed genuine." Elliot said. "It's looking like maybe there's nothing more to this than suicide. Sometimes people don't show signs of what they're really going through."

Tom grunted agreement, then looked away. "We'll still follow up with AJ."

"Oh yeah? How was that?" Elliot asked.

"Pretty much what I expected. Arrogant punk claiming ignorance. I've got him checking with his cronies for anything that might help us."

"Do you think he'll actually do it?"

"Yes."

Elliot waited for Tom to elaborate, but it was quickly clear that he would not. Intrigued, Elliot was about to push for more information when a knock sounded from the closed door.

"Come in," Tom shouted.

The door opened and revealed one of the front desk secretaries. She looked flustered and concerned. "I'm sorry to interrupt."

"Not at all," Elliot said. "What can we do for you?"

"We just received a call from the campus police. They received a report of violence in one of our dorms and asked that we notify you."

Elliot's brow arched. "Violence in a dorm? They think it's related to our case?"

The secretary cleared her throat. "Yes, sir. The person assaulted was Tonya Sheffield. A girl on her floor called it in, stating Tonya was being assaulted by a middle-aged couple in her dorm room. The couple had gone by the time our campus police arrived, but Tonya told them the couple were Emily Lancaster's parents."

"Shit," Tom growled. His chair screeched against the floor as he pushed it back. He jumped up and lumbered out of the room.

Elliot was on his feet and moving after his partner. "What's the address of the dorm?"

The secretary hurried after them and recited an address from memory. Elliot thanked her and followed Tom out of the building.

"They were supposed to come to us first," Tom grumbled. "This is not good."

No, Elliot thought as they climbed in the car and sped away. *This is not good at all.*

CHAPTER 8

Evening had arrived, and Paul sat in bed, propped up against the wall, with a textbook open in his lap. With each passing minute, he felt slightly more relieved. His mind was still heavy with the weight of Emily's death and the interview with the detectives, but there was something else there now. Something he thought lost. He felt hope.

He tried to clear his mind and get back to work, but the textbook pages blurred and nothing was retained. Homework was going to have to wait for another day. With a sigh, he flipped the cover closed and tossed the book down on the bed. The rain had stopped, and he thought he might go for a walk to clear his mind. He swung his leg off the bed and stood just as the door opened, and Dex entered the room.

"Bro, this is wild!"

"What now?" Paul asked. He didn't think he could stand anymore drama.

"What do you mean, what?" Dex asked incredulously. "Have you been sleeping or something? Didn't you hear the sirens?"

At the mention of sirens, Paul stiffened, and his stomach instinctively twinged. "I've been here trying to study. I must have zoned out. What happened?"

"That girl's parents showed up and started throwing hands, dude!"

Paul didn't follow. "What? What girl's parents?"

"For fuck's sake, Paul. Emily's parents. The suicide girl you hooked up with? Remember?"

Paul's mouth dropped.

"Her parents came to identify the body and get her stuff. They went to her dorm room and flipped out on her roommate. Bunch of the girls saw it happen. Said the dad was shaking her around and the mom was swinging at her."

"Oh, my God. Tonya."

"Yeah, that's her. They had to call the cops. I guess the parents left when they heard the girls calling the cops."

"Did they catch them?"

"Not our campus cops. Those dipshits couldn't catch a cold. Too busy flirting with coeds at the donut shop. Those detectives here investigating found them. They were camped out in the chapel. Wild shit."

Paul held his head in his hands. *Poor Tonya. I've got to go see her.* Suddenly, he remembered the note in his pocket - Tonya's number. She'd given it to him outside the health center.

"Speaking of detectives," Dex said, "how did it go when you talked to them?"

Paul turned and searched his bed for his phone. He found it wedged underneath the pillow. "It went pretty well," he said., grabbing a hoodie from the closet and sliding it over his head. "You were right about going there."

"So, they believed you? That's great, man. Glad to hear it."

"Yeah. I gotta go see Tonya. I can't believe they attacked her."

"Wait, you know her roommate, too? Damn dog, you've been getting around."

"Shut up, Dex," Paul said. "It's not like that. I met her at the health center today. She's just as fucked up about all this as I am."

Dex threw up his hands in surrender. "Sorry, bro. Didn't mean to offend."

Paul waved him off. "I'm not mad. I just gotta get to her. I'll see you later."

He was out the door and dialing her number before Dex could respond. Paul's heart broke for Tonya as he listened anxiously to the digital ringing on the phone. After four rings, it went to voicemail.

Hey, this is Tonya. I can't talk right now, but if you leave a message, maybe I'll call you back. Maybe.

An automated voice instructed him to leave a message after the tone, but he hung up and switched to text message.

Tonya, it's Paul. I heard what happened. I'm so sorry. Can I come see you?

Hitting send, he made his way out of the dorm and headed across the quad. He wasn't sure which building Tonya was in, so he went in the general direction of the girl's dorms. He kept his phone in his hand, checking frequently to see if she had responded.

Halfway across the quad, his phone dinged.

Hathaway Hall. I'll meet you outside.

Tonya read Paul's message again, fighting back tears. She was alone for the moment, but the girls on her floor had been checking in on her frequently. They had stayed with her until the police arrived. At first it was the campus police, but later the detectives she had interviewed with had shown up. They were clearly upset and frustrated. Emily's parents had not contacted them when they arrived, instead going directly to the dorm. After some questioning, they found out the parents had gained access to the building when a resident walked outside. The detectives took a brief statement from her, then left to find the parents.

Since then, she found out the detectives had caught Emily's parents and taken them in for questioning. The campus police had asked if she wanted to press assault charges on them, but she had declined. Horrified as she was by what happened, in her heart she knew they were grieving parents who needed to lash out at someone. Tonya felt as much to blame as anyone. In her mind, she was a valid target.

For the last two hours, she had been in her bed, staring at the wall. The detectives and her friends had all urged her to call her parents and let them know what had happened, but she wasn't ready to do that. She didn't want to talk to anyone. At least, not until Paul texted her. When her phone rang with an unknown caller, she ignored it. Then the text came through. She read his message and realized she wanted to talk. She *needed* to talk. Paul was the only person who might understand how she felt. His guilt mirrored her own, and she desperately needed like-minded company.

Taking advantage of no one being in the room to check on her, she slipped quietly out and down the hall. If anyone saw her go, they didn't call out to her, and she didn't look back. She hurried down the stairwell at the end of the hall and stepped outside. The rain from earlier in the day had brought much cooler temperatures with it. She let the long sleeves of her oversized sweatshirt slide over her hands and crossed her arms tightly across her chest.

In the distance, she saw someone crossing the quad. The figure passed under a lamppost, and she could tell it was Paul. Nervously, she waited for him to approach, unsure of what to say. When he caught sight of her, he increased his pace and closed the distance quickly.

"Hey, Tonya," he said. His breath fogged in wisps. "I don't know what to say. I'm so sorry."

Tonya tried to reply. *Thank you* were the words she meant to say, but what came out was a miserable moan, and before she knew what was happening, she was sobbing uncontrollably.

Paul wrapped his arms around her and hugged her tightly. He said nothing else, and Tonya was grateful. Nothing he could say would change what had happened or make her feel any less vulnerable and shitty. She just needed someone who understood to be with her and help her ride the wave of crushing sadness.

When it was over, Tonya was unsure how much time had passed. Her tears had ceased, but her shoulders still lurched in response to the stimulus overload. Paul loosened his arms and stepped away. She looked at him, then let out a pitiful chuckle. A wide, wet circle covered the shoulder of his hoodie. "I soaked you. I'm sorry."

Paul glanced at the spot, smiled, and shook his head. "Don't sweat it. Do you want to go for a walk?"

"Yeah, I would like that."

Together, they strolled away from the dorm. Paul told her about his interview with the detectives. Tonya was relieved to hear they seemed to believe him. She told him about the encounter with Emily's parents and the hateful things they had said.

"Jesus," Paul said. "They sound like those fanatic nut-job cult people you see on documentaries."

"I know, and it makes me feel so bad for Emily. It's no wonder she was the way she was. Had I known her family life was like that, I never would have pushed her to go to the party."

"Don't go down that road again," Paul said. "You didn't know, and you had good intentions. Leave it at that. Don't torture yourself."

"You're right, and I'm trying. It's just hard not to feel guilty."

"I hear that," Paul replied.

Tonya nodded. She knew he felt it just as much as she did.

They spent most of the rest of the walk in a comfortable silence. When they arrived back at the entrance to her building, Paul hugged her again. She squeezed him back, appreciating the comfort of his shared sympathy.

"Call me tomorrow," he said. "I'm sure the cops won't let her parents near you again without them being there too, but if anything happens, I want to know."

"I will. Thank you, Paul. For everything."

"Yeah, of course."

He let her go and stepped back. She waved as he turned and headed back toward the other side of the quad, then went inside. She made it back to her room without running into anyone, for which she was thankful. Not that she didn't appreciate the support of her friends, but she needed a break from the attention. Paul had been an exception to that rule, and she felt better having spent time with him. Now, she was succumbing to an overwhelming wave of exhaustion.

Back in her room, she quickly changed into shorts and a tank top and slid into bed. Sleep found her shortly after, and she dreamed of Emily.

CHAPTER 9

AJ Beaumont lay on the bed and watched the girl stroll around his bedroom, picking through books and movies on the shelves, his eyes glued to her ass. Her name was Katrina - *Katrina with a K, as she was quick to point out* - and she was one of a handful of girls AJ had gotten friendly with over the first few months of the school year. She wore tight, black denim shorts cut high enough that her cheeks were visible through the fishnet leggings she wore underneath and a black tank top. She always wore black, including her raven black hair she kept pulled back in a ponytail.

Katrina fit the goth stereotype, but there was nothing fake about it. She was genuine in her fascination with the occult, horror media, and metal music. Upon her arrival, she had immediately switched his playlist to some Satanic pop metal band. The current song was about rats. AJ wasn't a metal guy, but he admitted this stuff was catchy as hell. He wouldn't have dared to say otherwise, regardless. She could listen to and do whatever she wanted.

Katrina was fucking hot. AJ had been trying to hook up with her since the night he met her, but she was not an easy one to crack. He respected that, and found the more time he spent trying to put moves on her, the more he had grown to like her. She was a smart ass and had a deeply dark sense of humor, but he was into it.

After the visit from the detective that afternoon, AJ had been furious. Twice he had his dad's number pulled up on his phone, ready to pull some strings and see if he couldn't rattle that asshole's cage a bit. Both times, he had held back. There had been something off about the guy - an intensity that scared AJ and gave him pause. Here, his gut feeling was it was a dangerous move to retaliate. But he also was too pissed off to cooperate. Instead of calling up some of his buddies he knew were at the party, he crumpled up the dick's card and tossed it in the trash.

"Why don't you come over and snuggle up, babe?" AJ asked.

"Do I look like a girl that snuggles?" Katrina asked? "You mean you want me to come over there and rub your cock?"

"Your idea, not mine," AJ said with a sly grin.

"I want to get into some shit."

AJ frowned. "What do you mean?"

"We've got an opportunity tonight."

"Yes we do," AJ said.

"You're such a fucking perv," she said, rolling her eyes. "No, dick, the spirits are moving tonight."

AJ shook his head and grabbed his pipe from the bedside table. He took a hit, then offered it to Katrina. "What the hell are you going on about?"

Katrina snatched the pipe and took a hit. "That girl that killed herself. Trauma like that is a gateway to the spirits."

"Ok?"

"Those don't come along all the time. We have to seize the moment."

"And what does that mean?"

"It means we need to go there and try to communicate."

AJ stared at her with dull confusion. He wasn't sure if the weed hit that hard or if she was fucking with him. "You're serious?"

"Fuck yeah, I'm serious. Look," she said, snatching the knapsack she'd brought with her off the floor. She opened it up and pulled out a ouija board.

"Dude, you're crazy. I'm not using a ouija board in my house."

"Not here, dumbass. At the tower. The gateway will be the strongest where she killed herself."

"Okay, then even more of a no. I'm not going to the bell tower to talk to spirits with a ouija board."

"Come on, you pussy," Katrina said. She took another hit from the pipe, then handed it back. In the same motion, she slid her leg over his and straddled him.

Immediately, AJ felt himself harden, and he instinctively put his hands on her hips. His pulse quickened, and he shifted his hips to press into her.

"Come with me," she said, smiling coyly. "This is my shit, man. Do something for me, and maybe I'll do something for you."

AJ gasped as she ground her hips forward.

"Fuck me," he moaned. "Fine. Let's go."

"Yes!" Katrina shouted. She hopped off him and slid her phone from her back pocket. "I'm gonna have Vicky meet us there."

"Whoa, who the hell is Vicky?"

"She's my friend, and she wants to go, too. We already talked about it."

Fuck, AJ thought. He had a bad feeling he was going to end up getting duped on this deal. *Hundred bucks says she goes back to her place with her friend.*

Katrina seemed to read his mind. "Don't be a bitch, AJ. She's cool. Hell, she might come back here with us. If you're into that?"

AJ's eyes widened, and he tried not to let the surprise show on his face. "Whatever. Let's just get this over with."

The things you do to get laid.

Forty-five minutes later, they were approaching the bell tower. The night was chilly, but thankfully the rain and cloud cover had moved out, letting the moonlight guide their way. When they rounded the corner of the tower, AJ saw a girl leaning against the structure. She was nothing like he expected.

Vicky was a thin girl in baggy sweatpants and a long sleeve pullover. She had shoulder-length blond hair pulled back in two tight braids, one on each side. She looked like a soccer player, not a goth chick.

"Vicky!" Katrina shouted. "You ready for this, bitch?"

"I'm nervous," Vicky said. She kept casting quick glances at AJ.

Picking up on her discomfort, he reached out a hand. "I'm AJ. Nice to meet you."

"Vicky," she said, grasping his hand weakly, then quickly letting it drop.

"He's cool," Katrina said. "Bit of a douche, but aren't they all?"

AJ chuckled. "Fuck you."

"That's what he wants to do," Katrina said. "By the way, I told him we might go back to his place and fuck him for coming out here with us."

Vicky's mouth dropped, and she blushed violently. "Excuse me?"

"A little threesome action after we talk to the spirit world. That shit gets me hot."

"Absolutely not," Vicky said. She looked at AJ. "No offense, dude, but absolutely not."

AJ threw up his hands. "Wasn't my idea. No offense taken."

"You're a bitch, Katrina," Vicky said.

"I know. Now let's do this. We need to be discrete. Cops might still monitor the scene. I mean, we're not doing anything illegal, but let's not risk the hassle."

"We could not risk any hassle by not being here," AJ said. "This is dumb."

"It's not dumb, and your chances are not improving if you're gonna be cynical. Non-believers will slow our progress. Have an open mind."

AJ looked over at Vicky, who stood nervously with her arms wrapped tightly across her chest. "You're really into this shit? You don't seem the type."

"Because I don't look like her?" Vicky asked with annoyance. "Just because I'm not goth doesn't mean I don't believe in other realms of existence."

"Fine, I wasn't trying to offend. I'll behave. Let's just get this over with. Do your thing."

Katrina dropped to one knee and slid the bag from her shoulders. She reached inside and retrieved the ouija board. AJ glanced at Vicky, who watched Katrina intently. Katrina placed the board on the ground, then removed the planchette from the bag. It was made of auburn colored wood with intricate inlays carved around the edges and a hole carved in the center. She placed the planchette on the board, then looked up.

"Here we go."

Vicky stepped around the board and dropped to her knees, positioning herself to Katrina's right. AJ shook his head, then followed suit and knelt to Katrina's left. *What the fuck am I doing?*

"You guys know the rules, right?"

"Yes," Vicky said.

"Is this the one where you get two hundred dollars if you pass go?" AJ asked with a wry smile.

"Jesus," Vicky whispered.

"Seriously, dude. If you fuck this up, I'll zip tie your balls to a cactus. Getting into my pants will be way down on your list of priorities."

"Ouch," AJ said.

"This is serious, and there are rules."

"Okay, I'm not being a dick. I'm just saying, they sell these things at Walmart next to Guess Who and Clue. How serious can it be?"

"If you know what you're doing, it's as serious as it gets," Vicky said.

AJ studied her for a moment. The girl was intense, and he realized there was something different about her interest here than Katrina's usual otherworld bullshit. This was *important* for Vicky, but AJ couldn't fathom why. He only knew that she was not in the mood for jokes and if he wanted to stay on her good side, then he needed to cooperate.

"Alright, fine. I do not know the rules. What are they?"

"Keep your hands on the planchette, gently touching it. You're not pushing it. We ask questions, and we don't play games. No joking around. Don't break contact with the planchette and never end a session without saying goodbye," Katrina said.

"Why not?"

"If you don't say goodbye, the spirit still has access to this world. You open yourself up for possession," Vicky said.

AJ locked eyes with her again and saw no trace of humor. She believed it. He fought back the urge to respond with a Linda Blair joke and simply nodded. "Okay, got it. Always say goodbye."

Katrina scanned the area for anybody walking nearby. Satisfied that they were alone, she nodded. "Let's begin." She gingerly put her fingertips on the planchette. Vicky followed, then AJ. The wood felt warm under his fingers, and he suddenly felt uncomfortable. He had never believed in this shit, and he would not start now, but something felt off. His skin prickled with goosebumps. *Just get it over with. An hour from now, I'll be back in my room, hopefully with Katrina.*

Katrina cleared her throat and closed her eyes. "Is anyone here with us?"

CHAPTER 10

*T*onya tossed and turned on her bed. Her blanket had fallen to the floor, and in her sleep, she had pulled the sheet loose and wrapped it around herself. A whimper sounded from her throat and her leg kicked out.

In her dream, she was being chased down a dark hallway. Two figures pursued her. She couldn't see them; they were shadows in the dark. But she could hear them clearly.

"Harlot!"

"Deceiver!"

"Servant of the fallen angel!"

She cried out, begging for them to leave her alone. The hollow voices of Emily's parents echoed in her ears.

"To the pit with you, foul creature!"

As she ran down the endless hallway, she passed closed doorways, each with window panes allowing a view of the interior. Most of them were dark, but in some she could see glowing red eyes flashing back at her.

"I'm sorry," she shouted. "Please, forgive me."

"No forgiveness!"

"You shall be judged!"
Tonya screamed and kept running.

At first, nothing happened. AJ glanced at Katrina. Her eyes were still closed, and she sat perfectly still. Vicky mimicked Katrina, though AJ noted a quiver in her jaw.

"If you are here, please make yourself known. We want to talk to you," Katrina said.

Another moment of silence.

"Guess the spirits aren't home?" AJ said. He heard Katrina's sharp intake of breath, and prepared to be berated again, when the bell tower clanged to life. All three of them jumped.

"Jesus Chris," AJ said, then exhaled slowly. His heartbeat hammered in his chest.

"Put your hands back," Vicky hissed. "That was a sign."

AJ rolled his eyes. "That was a sign that it's midnight. The bells ring every hour."

"Oh yeah," Katrina said with a grin. "Check your watch, AJ."

Confused, AJ flipped his wrist and the Apple Watch face lit up.

11:47 PM

A chill ran through him and he looked back at the girls with wide eyes. "Okay, that's fucking weird."

"Put your hands back on the planchette," Katrina said.

AJ did as he was told.

Detective Tom Stone sat in his hotel room. Papers were scattered across the small desk next to his notebook. An open bottle of Maker's Mark, now nearly half gone, sat next to a paper cup and a bucket of melting ice he had filled at the ice machine down the hall.

He was brooding. The disaster with the girl's parents ate at him. They never should've gained access to the dorm without an escort. He thought of the traumatized girl; the roommate, Tonya. Tom had been a bit of a hard ass with her in the interview, and he regretted it. He hadn't realized it then, but he had already been projecting his own biased feeling about this case onto her. Even before he snapped on the Beaumont kid, it was influencing his actions.

The dead girl just reminded him so goddamn much of his own daughter. It was too close to home, and he needed to blame someone. He didn't want it to be a suicide. If Emily could do it, his daughter could do it, too.

He grabbed the cup off the desk and threw back the remaining bourbon, then scooped ice into the glass and poured more from the bottle. He imagined his wife's disapproval if she could see him right now, but he was beyond caring.

He took a slow sip and thought about Emily.

"Was that you? Did you make the bells ring?" Katrina asked.

AJ gasped as the planchette moved suddenly. The felt pads glued to the bottom of the wood made a soft hissing sound as it moved. It circled the board in a wide figure-eight pattern, then stopped on YES.

"Thank you for talking to us," Katrina said. "What is your name?"

The planchette came to life and swooped quickly from letter to letter.

E-M-I-L-Y

"It's her," Vicky whispered.

AJ swallowed hard. "Are you guys fucking with me?"

"No," they both said in unison.

He believed them.

"Emily," Katrina said, "did you kill yourself here? Did you jump off the tower?"

The planchette glided around the board.

YES

"Why?" Vicky asked. "Why did you do it?"

The response was frantic; the planchette raced across the board, nearly clipping off the edge on multiple occasions.

I-A-M-A-S-I-N-N-E-R

"IAMASINNER?" AJ asked in confusion, pronouncing it as one word. "IAM ASSINER?"

"Holy shit," Katrina said.

"What?" AJ asked.

"I know what she's trying to say."

Vicky spoke for her. "I am a sinner."

Dex's eye snapped open at the sound of Paul's shout. He jerked upright in bed and squinted through the darkened dorm room at his roommate's bed. Paul groaned deeply, then twisted in his blanket. He could see his legs and bare feet sticking out the bottom of the covers and churning, as if he was scrambling away from something.

Wild ass dream, Dex thought to himself. "Yo, Paul. You good man?"

Paul did not react to Dex's voice. He continued to twist and groan and occasionally shout. Dex couldn't make out what he was saying, but there was definite fear in his voice.

Dex shook his head. He considered getting up and shaking him awake, then decided against it. Paul had been weird since the shit went down with that girl, and Dex was sure his subconscious was feeding him gnarly nightmares. He remembered hearing somewhere that you should never wake someone in the middle of a nightmare. Or maybe that was for sleepwalking? He wasn't sure, but either way, he figured it was safer to let Paul ride it out. As riled up as he seemed to be, Dex was worried Paul might throw hands at him if he shook him awake. Best to leave him be.

Dex dropped back onto the pillow and pulled his own blanket up over the side of his head, then turned so his back was to Paul's side of the room. After a couple minutes of listening to Paul's protests, he rolled back over and retrieved his earbuds from the bedside table. He slipped them in his ears, activated the noise canceling function and queued up a Spotify mix of relaxation sounds. The first track was the sound of steady rainfall pattering against a tin roof. He exhaled deeply and let the rain return him to sleep.

"Why do you think you're a sinner?" Katrina asked.

The planchette glided around the board, picking up speed. It stopped only for a split second on each letter.

"I can't keep up with it," AJ said.

"Can you please slow down? We don't understand what you're telling us," Vicky said.

The planchette quivered beneath their fingertips, then lurched back into action. This time, it moved directly to each letter, no longer drawing figure eights between each stop. It was still fast, but the directness allowed them to catch the letters.

L-U-S-T

C-O-V-E-T

S-I-N

"You killed yourself because you lusted for someone?" Katrina's mouth turned down in a sad frown. "You didn't have to do that, Emily. Everyone lusts. It's just human nature."

The planchette shot to the corner of the board.

NO

"Hell, I lust every day," AJ said, then winked at Katrina.

The planchette moved again.

S-I-N-N-E-R Y-O-U A-R-E- A- S-I-N-N-E-R - Y-O-U A-R-E A-L-L S-I-N-N-E-R-S

"Wow," Vicky said.

"So, should we jump off the tower, too?" AJ asked. He rolled his eyes. "This is fucking stupid. Which one of you is doing this?"

"We're not, asshole," Katrina hissed.

D-E-A-T-H

The three of them fell silent.

P-R-I-C-E O-F S-I-N I-S D-E-A-T-H

Elliot Lyons stepped out of his hotel room onto the small balcony. He couldn't sleep. His mind ran the day's events on a continuous loop, and he couldn't turn it off. He leaned against the railing, starting at the damp coldness on his bare forearms.

The hotel was on the outskirts of campus. From his room on the third floor, he could vaguely see the outlines of the campus buildings. They all blended together into a seamless tapestry of brick facades. The only identifiable landmark was the bell tower, standing ominously in the distance. Bathed in moonlight, it reminded Elliot of a gothic tower from one of the old seventies horror movies he used to watch when he was a kid. He could imagine Vincent Price or Christopher Lee perched at the top of the tower, glowering down at the surroundings.

Was that how it had looked to Emily? Had she chosen to jump from the tower because it looked like a place where people go to die?

Of course not. He scolded himself for his flight of morbid fancy. She chose it because it was the highest place on campus to jump from. It was a tragic end to a troubled young woman. That's it.

He wanted to believe that, but his gut begged to differ. Something gnawed at his mind. There was more to this.

Damned if he knew what it was, though.

"The price of a sin is death." Vicky looked nervously at Katrina. "I think we need to stop now."

"Agreed," AJ chimed in, though he didn't base his approval on the fear gripping Vicky's face.

Katrina glanced back and forth between them, then nodded. "Yeah, it's getting a little heavy." She paused, then straightened her posture. "Thank you, Emily, for talking to us. We're sorry about what happened to you. We have to go now. Goodbye."

NO

The planchette soared, digging into the board. Vicky's eyes widened in terror. Katrina watched their hands speed around the board in mesmerized fascination, her mouth hanging agape.

"Stop it, Kat," AJ said. "It's enough."

"Katrina!" Vicky shouted.

Katrina blinked hard and shook her head. "Goodbye, Emily." She let go of the planchette. The others followed her lead. The planchette coasted to a stop, then tipped over the edge of the board, landing upside down on the sidewalk.

"Jesus Christ," Vicky said.

Paul opened his eyes and bolted upright in his bed. A ragged scream tore from his throat.

The bell tower came to life, tolling midnight.

CHAPTER 11

P aul sat perched atop a cushioned stool in the small coffee shop off Marigold Street on the edge of campus. A cup of French vanilla cappuccino sat in front of him, wisps of steam trailing through the small opening of the lid. He glanced outside at the sidewalk. Tonya was supposed to meet him for coffee at two o'clock. He picked up his phone and saw 2:15pm. She hadn't texted, but it was no surprise. Not the lack of communication or her being late.

It had been two weeks since Emily's suicide. The investigation had run its course. Detectives Lyons and Stone had determined there was no foul play involved. Detective Lyons had called Paul to let him know they were closing the investigation and thanked him for his cooperation.

At the beginning, those words would have felt like the weight of the world being lifted off his body. He was relieved, but it had done little to change his mood.

Those goddamn nightmares.

Paul had not had a good night's sleep since the night of Emily's suicide. The first few nights were to be expected, but ever since the day he talked to the detectives, he'd suffered through terrible nightmares. Every single night he woke in terror, covered in sweat, and panting from exhaustion. His muscles were tired and sore, as if he'd run a marathon. He could see the impact of the nightmares on his face as well. Every time he passed a mirror, the exhaustion in his eyes was more apparent.

Dex was the only person who knew about the dreams, though Paul had not divulged the full details. Whenever Dex would question him about them, he would claim he didn't remember. Paul was sure Dex didn't believe that, but his roommate was kind enough to let it be. After two weeks of tormented nights, he'd finally decided it was time to talk to someone. He needed to talk to Tonya. If anyone would understand, it was her.

It had taken him an entire day of working up the courage to reach out to her. Despite the ease they had become friendly during the investigation, they hadn't spoken since. Paul thought of her constantly, but something held him back from texting her. At first, the bond of their shared experience had been a relief. Now, it was a reminder of things they were trying to put behind them. At least, that was how Paul rationalized it. He thought Tonya must be feeling the same way. She had not reached out to him, either. When he finally sent the message asking her if she would meet with him for coffee, she responded immediately that she would.

Paul checked his watch again, and his stomach sank. She was twenty minutes late. *Maybe she changed her mind?*

The cafe door swung open and jingled the bell above it. Paul looked up to see Tonya walk through, and his mouth dropped. She looked ghostly pale in the dim lights of the cafe. Even from across the room, Paul could see dark pockets under her eyes. Her face had thinned, cheeks sunken in against her jaws. It had only been two weeks, but Paul guessed she must've lost at least ten pounds from her already slight frame.

Tonya met his gaze, then looked at the floor. Paul flinched, realizing his shock at her appearance must have been obvious. She hurried across the room and sat on the stool across from him, letting her bag drop to the floor beside her.

"I know," she said. "I look like shit."

"No," Paul said.

"Yes, I do," she replied, finally looking him in the eyes. "But you do, too, so I guess it's okay."

Paul stared back at her for a second, then chuckled. "Fair enough. Can I get you a drink?"

"Coffee. Black."

Paul nodded and slid off the stool. The barista met him at the counter and he ordered Tonya's drink. While he waited, he turned back to the table. Tonya stared at her hands, nervously rubbing her fingers together. He could see her knee bouncing under the table. The barista sat the cup of coffee in front of him, and he carried it back to the table.

"Thank you," Tonya said. She removed the cap and blew softly into the steam. "I've been living on this stuff."

"Same," Paul replied. He cleared his throat. "Thank you for coming. I'm sorry I didn't text you sooner. I thought about it a lot, but I think I thought we could use some time to let things settle down a bit, you know?"

"Yeah, totally. Don't worry about it. We've had a lot on our plates."

"Definitely," Paul said.

They lapsed into silence, both sipping at their drinks and looking nervously around the room. *Just tell her,* Paul thought.

"Are you doing okay?" Tonya asked, breaking the silence.

"Yeah," Paul said. *No, you're fucking not!*

Paul shook his head. "No, actually. That's a lie. I'm not doing okay."

Tonya stared at him. "Me either. I can't sleep. I've been having night-mares about what happened."

Paul had lifted his cup to take another sip, but his hand froze midway.

"I've been dreaming that I'm trapped in this hallway that just goes on and on forever. And Emily's parents are there chasing me. I never see them, but I hear them screaming at me."

Paul's hand quivered, and drops of cappuccino splashed onto the table.

"There are doors all down the hall, but I can't go in them because I have to keep running. And sometimes I see someone staring at me from the rooms when I go past. I see the eyes. Red eyes."

The cup slipped from Paul's hand, bounced off the table, and fell to the floor in a spray of creamy liquid and foam.

"Oh," Tonya said, as she slipped off the stool and away from the table. "I'm sorry, I..."

"Are you okay?" Tonya asked, her face filled with concern. "You look like you saw a ghost."

The barista approached the table with a damp cloth and began wiping up the spill.

"I'm sorry," Paul said. "I can clean it up."

"It's fine," the girl replied. "I got it. Happens all the time."

Paul detected a hint of annoyance in her tone and felt even worse. She quickly finished and returned to the counter.

"What happened?"

"This sounds crazy, but I've been having the same dreams. Every night."

"Are you serious?" Tonya's voice quivered.

"Yes. Well, except her parents aren't there in my dream. But someone is chasing me. But the endless hall, the closed doors, the red eyes watching, all of that is the same."

"Holy shit," Tonya murmured. "What does it mean?"

"I don't know."

"I mean, it has to have something to do with Emily. But how could we both be having the same dream? It's not possible."

"A month ago I would've said the same thing, but here we are."

Tonya fell silent.

"I don't know what to do. I've tried taking things; sleeping pills, gummies, even getting shit faced drunk. None of it helps. I still have nightmares and wake up feeling even worse."

"Have you noticed anything else strange? Like, when you're not asleep?"

Paul considered. "No, I don't think so. Have you?"

Tonya ran her hand over her forehead and squeezed her temples. "Maybe."

"Like what?"

Tonya looked up at him. "I think I've seen her."

"Her who?"

"Emily," Tonya replied. "I've been seeing Emily."

Paul paused and pondered her words. He knew immediately that his response would carry a lot of weight for Tonya. There was a desperation in her eyes begging for some kind of acknowledgement; whether that was belief, confirmation, or a logical explanation, Paul wasn't sure.

"You've been seeing Emily? Like you're seeing things that remind you of her?"

"No."

"You think you've been seeing her ghost?"

"I know how it sounds," Tonya said. "I don't believe in ghosts, but I swear I've seen her. Once or twice, I could've written it off as my imagination; maybe I saw a girl who looked like her. I'm trying to make myself believe that, but I don't think I can."

"Okay," Paul said, "where did you see her?"

"The first time, I was walking back to my dorm from here at the cafe, actually. I was across the street from the bell tower, and I looked at it and she was standing by the edge of the tower. She was watching me."

Paul shifted on his stool. "Look, I'm not being dismissive at all, but if you saw her from across the street, couldn't it have been someone else? Just some random girl hanging out by the tower?"

"That's exactly what I told myself. It creeped me the fuck out, but it had to be just a coincidence. Someone that looked a little like her from a distance. Obviously, I was thinking about her when I looked at the tower, so my mind just filled in the blank."

"Yeah, that's what I'm thinking."

"But then I saw her again. The next night, I was in my dorm. It was late, and I was going to the shower. There were some girls coming in together at the end of the hall and when I saw them, I saw her. She was standing behind them, staring down the hall at me."

"Did those girls see her?"

"I don't think so."

"I don't know, Tonya. You said it was late, right? Maybe you were just exhausted and your mind played tricks on you?"

Tonya cast her eyes down at the table, and her shoulders slumped. "Maybe."

"Listen, I swear I'm not trying to blow you off with this. It just can't be possible, right? She died, and it's weighing on both of us, but she's gone. It's not possible."

"Neither is us having the same nightmare every night," Tonya said flatly.

Paul didn't know what to say to that. She was right. They were having the same dream. She confirmed every detail without him telling anyone. Why was it so hard for him to accept this?

"Thank you for the coffee, Paul. It was nice to have someone to talk to. You're probably right. Not sleeping is wreaking havoc on my brain, and I'm hallucinating. I just need to sleep."

She stood and picked up her bag. "I'm gonna head back and try to rest. You should do the same."

Paul slid off his stool and walked with her toward the door. "I'm sorry if I upset you. Seriously, I don't want you to think I don't believe you. It's the opposite. I believe you, I just don't think you're actually seeing her ghost or whatever. It has to be your subconscious feeding images to your brain or something."

"Yeah, you're probably right," Tonya said. She pulled open the door and hurried outside. "Let's get together again in a few days. Hopefully, we're done dreaming by then." Before Paul could respond, she was walking away.

Paul watched her go. For a moment, he considered going after her, but thought better of it. She had played it cool, but he knew his efforts to debunk her visions hurt her. *Just give her some time,* he thought. The shock of everything would wear off eventually, and things would get back to normal.

CHAPTER 12

Dex tapped his ID card against the small black reader mounted beside the door of the dormitory. A green light flashed and the locking mechanism snapped open, granting access. He stepped inside and tapped his earbud, resuming the blast of early 2000s pop punk. He passed through the deserted front lobby and into the stairwell.

He emerged into the third-floor hallway and made his way down toward his room. Noise from televisions and Bluetooth speakers floated out of a few open doorways, but the hall itself was empty of traffic as well. Dex made a mental note of it, but it wasn't completely unusual for a weeknight.

Upon reaching the door of his room, he turned the knob, but found it locked. *Paul must be out somewhere,* he thought as he fished the key from his pocket. He pushed the key into the lock, turned it, and shouldered his way through the door.

The light was off and deep shadows cloaked the room, but Dex could see Paul standing across the room, facing his bed. "What are you doing there in the dark, buddy?" His mind flashed back to the locked door, and he grinned. "Did I just catch you jerkin' it?"

Paul remained silent and motionless.

"Yo, Paul?"

Slowly, the shadowy figure turned, revealing strands of long, dark hair hanging loosely around a pale face. Dex flinched backward.

"Whoa, hey," Dex stammered. "Who are you?"

The girl turned silently back toward the bed.

"Are you a friend of Paul's? Did he leave you here?"

"This is a bed of sin." Her voice was a crackled whisper, like dry leaves blowing along the ground.

Dex stared at the girl with growing discomfort. This chick was weird. Why the fuck would Paul bring her here? He realized how dark the room was and inched toward the light switch on the wall. He froze when she spoke again.

"Seduction of the innocent."

"I'm sorry," Dex said. "I don't know what you're talking about."

The girl turned and moved gracefully across the room toward the door. She wore a long dress that pooled around her feet and slid across the wood with a gentle wisp of soft fabric. She kept her face forward and down, letting her dark hair hang like curtains around her face. Dex cringed away from her as she approached. When she reached the threshold of the doorway, she stopped.

"Are you a sinner?"

"Excuse me?"

The girl repeated the question again without turning toward him.

"Are you a sinner?"

"I...don't think so."

The girl stood motionless; the yellow light from the hallway splashed into the room against the lower half of her dress. Her chalk white arms hung limply at her sides, but her fingers held clawed handfuls of the white fabric.

"You lie," she whispered, then stepped into the hall and out of sight.

Dex stood there, unable to process the encounter. "What the actual fuck was that?" He flipped the wall switch, bathing the room in fluorescent light, then poked his head out into the hall.

The girl was already gone.

Dex sat waiting, propped up against his headboard, when Paul entered the room thirty minutes later.

"Dude."

Paul emptied his pockets onto the desk and flopped onto the bed. "What?"

"What the fuck?"

Paul propped himself up on his elbow and looked at Dex with confusion. "What?"

"Who the fuck was that girl?"

"What girl?"

"Don't give me that shit, bro. That creepy chick you left in here."

Paul stared at him for a moment. "I don't know what you're talking about. What girl?"

"That's what I'm asking you, asshole. Next time you bring home a weirdo and decide to bail, don't leave her for me to deal with?"

Paul shook his head and sat up, sliding his legs over the edge of the bed, and leaned forward. "I didn't have a girl here today. I went to the coffee shop and met Tonya, but I didn't bring her here. And she's not weird."

Dex shook his head. "Don't fuck with me, dude. I'm not in the mood."

"I'm not fucking with you. What are you talking about?"

"When I got back tonight, there was a girl in our room. She was just standing there by your bed...in the dark. And the door was locked."

"What? How the hell did she get in here?"

"Because you brought her here, then left?"

"Dex, I did not bring a girl here today. Did she say who she was?"

"No, she said a bunch of creepy shit, then left. And apparently ran away because I looked in the hallway and she was gone already."

"What did she say?"

"Well, she said your bed was a bed of sin, something about the seduction of the innocent or some shit, and then she asked me if I was a sinner?"

Paul's brow crinkled in confusion. "I don't know, man. She wasn't with me."

"Then how did she get in with the door locked?"

"Beats me. I guess we should report it to the RA."

Dex got up from the bed and paced the room. "You think she swiped a key or something?"

"Maybe. You're really not messing with me?"

"No, dude. And if you're fucking with me, you're doing a hell of a job."

"Swear to God, Dex. I was out with Tonya this evening. Before that, I was here by myself and in class before that."

"Fine. Then it's extra creepy. I'm going to tell Brad about it now. You wanna come with me?"

"No, go ahead. I think Brad's a little annoyed with me, anyway. I heard from some guys he's pissed about me being involved with the Emily thing. Dude takes his role as resident advisor pretty seriously. Doesn't want any bad press on his floor."

"Oh yeah. What a douche," Dex said. He crossed the room and was almost through the door when a thought occurred to him and he paused. "You know what, I never met that Emily chick, but I saw the picture of her on the news. The weird girl that was in here kind of looked like her. Weird, right?"

Paul stared back at him, color draining from his face. "Yeah," he said after a long pause, "that is weird."

Dex eyed him curiously, but let it go. Paul had been acting strangely ever since the shit went down. He was getting used to it. "Okay, I'll let you know what the resident douche has to say."

As he left the room, he glanced back at Paul, still staring after him. The guy was white as a sheet. *Fucking weird,* Dex thought. *I can't wait for everyone to stop being weird.*

CHAPTER 13

"Come on, babe. You haven't been over in like a week. What's the deal?"

AJ lay back on his bed with the phone on speaker on his lap, waiting for Katrina to reply. He'd called and texted her multiple times a day, but she had not come back to see him since the night at the bell tower.

"Lay off, dick. I haven't felt great."

"Well, come on over and let me make you feel better. They don't call me Dr. Love for no reason."

"No one calls you that."

"You could be the first!"

"You're an idiot," Katrina replied, but her tone softened. "Can I be real with you?"

"Of course," AJ said.

"The whole ouija board thing kind of fucked me up."

"Don't worry about it, Kat. It's all bullshit. I know you act like you believe all this shit, but tell me, deep down in your heart, you don't really believe we were talking to a fucking ghost?"

"I know I wasn't moving it, and I trust Vicky. And she's even more fucked about it than I am."

"What do you mean?"

"I saw her the other day, and she looked like a train wreck. Doesn't look like she's slept in days."

"Well, did you ask her about it?"

"Of course. I'm not a selfish asshole."

"Neither am I."

"Are you sure about that?"

"Ouch. Why do you always go so hard on me? Yes, I like to party, and I get a little wild sometimes. I can even be a little abrasive. But I genuinely think you are a cool chick. You're fine as hell, and I'm not gonna stop trying to win you over, but I wouldn't put in all this effort if all I wanted was a hookup. This is me being real with you, okay?"

Katrina was silent for a moment, then chuckled. "Well, look at you being all vulnerable. That's adorable."

"Don't push it," AJ replied, but a smile lit up his face. "Come over, and let's talk about it."

"Can I bring Vicky?"

AJ rolled his eyes. Despite Katrina's tease from the week before, a little three-way action with Vicky was definitely off the table. "I guess so, if you think she'll even want to come. I don't think she liked me very much."

"Can't blame her there," Katrina replied.

"See, there you go again, and after I was so sweet to you."

"Shut up, AJ. I'll call Vicky and see if she'll come. It would be good for us to talk through it. Maybe it will help both of us."

"Sounds like a plan. I'm gonna go jump in the shower. See you in an hour?"

"Yeah. PS, I'm not fucking you, so keep your dick in your pants."

"Yes, ma'am," AJ replied, not without a playful hint of sorrow in his voice.

"I didn't say never," Katrina replied, letting the syllables in *never* drag out. "Just not tonight."

"Whatever you say, Kat. See you soon."

AJ ended the call, leaped from the bed, and hurried to the shower. In his excitement, he did not notice the dark figure standing in the hall just outside his open bedroom door.

Katrina listened to the phone ring four times before the voicemail message played. *Hi, this is Vicky. Leave me a message.* There was a pause and then a beep. "Answer your fucking phone, bitch!"

Immediately after ending the call, she rapidly typed another text message to Vicky.

If you don't answer the phone, I'll come over and kick your door in. Don't think I can't do it. These legs are lethal.

The message delivered, and Katrina tossed the phone down onto the bed in frustration. She stalked across her room and checked her makeup. As much as she tried to go with the flow, she couldn't deny the worry lines creasing her forehead. Something was definitely wrong with Vicky. The whole thing at the bell tower had been really strange. Katrina had taken part in plenty of seances over the last few years; some of them were bullshit, but she believed some of her experiences were authentic. That night was one of those. AJ was a tool, but she didn't peg him as someone who would fake a ouija board session. He didn't believe in it at all. He would've wanted nothing to happen, so it made no sense for him to fake it.

Maybe Vicky was so bothered because she had never seen it work that well before? Katrina knew Vicky had done it before, so maybe she just wasn't as ready as she thought for the real deal? Katrina felt a tinge of guilt. Communicating with the dead was heavy stuff. She always made sure the people with her at a seance were comfortable and prepared. Now, she wondered if she had assumed too much about Vicky's experience and let the poor girl walk into a wildly successful seance without being mentally ready to handle it.

From behind her, the phone vibrated on the bed. She grabbed it up and looked at the screen. "Finally," she said with relief, then answered.

"Bitch, what's your deal?"

"Hi, Kat."

"You've been avoiding me, and I've seen you. You look like you caught the black plague. What's going on?"

There was a pause and crackling static on the other end of the line, then Vicky replied, "I'm not feeling well."

"I can tell. Did you go see a doctor?"

"No," Vicky replied. Her voice was lifeless, as if she were talking in her sleep. "I'm not sick like that."

Katrina sighed. "It's about the other night, isn't it? Listen, Vicky. I'm sorry it got so out of hand. I've never had a session get that crazy. If I had known what would happen, I would have prepared you better."

"You didn't know."

"I know that, but I still feel guilty. And now look at you. Girl, we need to get you out of your room and back to normal. I'm going to see AJ to talk about what happened. Truthfully, I've been struggling with it, too. I think it could help us if we talk about it. Will you come with me?"

"I don't want to," Vicky said.

"Please, bitch, do it for me. Let me help you."

Vicky was silent again. Were it not for the soft static, Katrina would have thought she had hung up.

"Please, Vicky?"

"Fine. But it won't matter."

"It will matter. Communicating with the dead is a serious thing. It can mess you up sometimes. We just need to come to peace with what happened; talk it out and then we can move on."

"We didn't just talk to her."

Katrina frowned. "What do you mean?"

"You were there. When we tried to say goodbye, she said no. We didn't close the door, and now she's free to come and go as she pleases."

"Vicky, honey, it doesn't work that way."

"If that's what you think, then you don't know as much as you think you do."

Katrina blanched in surprise. Vicky had never spoken to her like this. Her instinct to fire back was intense, but she bit her lip and fought it back. "We'll talk about it. I'll come get you, and we'll go together, okay?"

"Fine."

"See you in a—"

The phone disconnected. Katrina pulled it away from her ear and stared at the screen. *What the fuck has gotten into her?* She dropped the phone back to the bed and went to finish getting ready. Vicky's words replayed through her mind while she touched up her makeup and gathered her things.

She's free to come and go as she pleases.

CHAPTER 14

AJ stood in the shower with his head down, letting the spray soak his hair and stream down his back. A speaker on the bathroom counter blasted a playlist of early 2000s rock. AJ's head bobbed with the beat while he rinsed the shampoo from his hair. Then he lathered up his body, giving extra attention to the downstairs area. He didn't expect to get anywhere with Katrina tonight, but he was taking no chances.

Disturbed roared through the speaker as he turned off the water, encouraging him to get up and get down with the sickness. That song always got him fired up, and he banged his head while he toweled off. He slid on a pair of boxer briefs and applied deodorant, then rummaged through his dresser.

"Fuck." Most of his clothes were downstairs in the laundry room. He glanced at the clock on his nightstand. He only had maybe twenty or thirty minutes before the girls would show up. With a groan, he set off through the house toward the basement staircase. The house was gloomy and cloaked with shadows. AJ flipped on light switches as he passed through each room. When he made it to the basement stairwell, he took the stairs two at a time and rounded the corner at the landing.

His finger wrapped around the chain dangling from the lightbulb, but his hand froze.

Across the room, a dark shape loomed next to the washing machine. AJ could tell from the shape that it was a girl, even though its back was turned to him. Long, dark hair lay in tangles down the back of a black dress.

"Jesus Fuck," AJ exclaimed. "Who the fuck are you?"

The figure remained motionless.

"Hey bitch, this is my house. How did you get in here?" His voice shook with fear and anger. Realizing his finger was still wrapped around the light chain, he pulled it sharply. The bulb grew bright, then popped in a dazzling flash, blinding him with a white haze. He blinked, trying to clear his vision. When his eyes adjusted back to the gloom of the basement, the figure was gone.

AJ twisted around and scanned the room. The basement was full of random junk and shadows dominated every visible section of wall, but nothing that resembled a person.

Did you imagine that shit?

He stood still, listening for any sound of movement or breathing in the dark. His heart hammered in his chest, and he took slow breaths to calm himself. *Get it together,* he thought. *You're freaking yourself out.*

After another tense moment of silence, he shook his head and hurried over to the dryer. He pulled open the lid and a tunnel of yellow light spilled out onto the floor. Leaning over, he pulled handfuls of clothes out of the machine and into the basket at his feet. He glanced at the red light glowing on the washing machine, showing the load was finished, but left it. The girls would be there soon, and he wanted to get the hell out of the basement.

With a grunt, he scooped up the laundry basket and hurried across the room to the stairs. As he rounded the corner and put his foot on the first step, a loud creak echoed down the stairwell and he watched in confusion as the door at the top of the stairs closed; the light from the hall became a shrinking sliver until it vanished and cast him into total darkness.

Behind him, the sound of a cloth rustling emanated from somewhere in the room, followed by a hoarse whisper.

Sinner.

Katrina pulled the car over to the curb in front of AJ's house and killed the engine. Vicky sat quietly in the passenger seat. Katrina had tried to make small talk while they drove, but Vicky was stoic and wouldn't engage. After a few yes or no answers with no elaboration, Katrina gave up. At least she had gotten her to come along. The poor girl looked even worse than the last time Katrina had seen her.

"Come on," Katrina said, as she climbed out of the car.

Vicky got out of the car and looked up at the house. "Doesn't look like he's home."

Katrina followed her gaze to the house. "That's weird," she said. All the windows were dark. "I know he's here. He better not be fucking with us. Now is not the time to be funny."

"No," Vicky agreed. "It's not." She stared at the house, then turned toward Katrina. Her eyes were wide and bright, reflecting the glow of the overhead streetlight. "I think something bad is happening."

"What do you mean?" Katrina asked. The way Vicky spoke sent an icy chill rippling down her spine. She was acting so strange, and it left Katrina feeling unsettled.

Vicky turned back to the house. "Something bad is happening in there."

Katrina walked around the car and stood next to Vicky. "Why do you think that?"

"I can feel it," Vicky replied. "I can feel *her*."

"You're scaring me, V."

Vicky turned and locked eyes with Katrina. "You should be scared. We all should be." Then she trudged up the sidewalk to the front porch.

Katrina hurried after her. "Vicky, please. I think you're taking this too far. AJ is fine. You'll see. I guarantee you he's hiding in there waiting to pop out and say boo like a dipshit."

Vicky didn't respond. She stopped at the door and waited for Katrina. Katrina raised a fist to knock, then decided against it. "Fuck it, we're invited." She grabbed the doorknob and pushed it open.

Somewhere in the house, AJ screamed.

Katrina tensed and grabbed Vicky's arm. Then she groaned in exasperation. "Real fucking cute, dickhead." She ushered Vicky into the house with her and flipped on the light switch by the door. The entry hall blazed into light. "If you wanted us to come and hang for a while, this is the worst possible way to start!" she shouted. "Stop being a douche and come out. We're not playing hide and seek with you."

AJ screamed again.

"Fuck," Katrina whispered.

"It's not a joke," Vicky said. "Something bad is happening."

Katrina ignored Vicky's warning, choosing not to let her mind go down that road. She took a few steps further into the house. "AJ, I'm serious. Stop being stupid and come out or we're leaving."

"Help me!" AJ's voice cracked and strained with the power of his scream. "PLEASE!"

Katrina walked slowly down the entry hall toward where she thought the screams were coming from. Her chest was tight with apprehension and her breathing came in rapid, short bursts. AJ's last cries for help contained genuine fear. She didn't believe he could fake that much emotion. It sounded raw and primal. "Where are you?"

A heavy thump sounded from below them, followed by a howl of pain. "Please help me," AJ cried. His shouts were weaker now.

Katrina stood frozen in the hall, fear pinning her in place. Vicky stepped up beside her and put a firm hand on her back. "I think he's downstairs. Where are the basement stairs?"

"I don't know," Katrina said. "I've never...I don't know." Her eyes welled with warm tears as she stared helplessly at Vicky. "I don't know what to do. What's happening?"

Vicky pushed past her and started opening doors. First was a closet. The second, a half bathroom. The third and final door on the hall before it ended into the kitchen wouldn't open. Unfazed, she tried again. The knob turned freely, but the door wouldn't budge. She turned and shouted at Katrina. "Help me push."

Katrina nodded and rushed down the hall. She placed herself to the side of Vicky, then in unison, they rammed their shoulders into the door. It burst free of the doorframe, nearly sending Vicky tumbling down the stairs. Katrina wrangled her in with an arm around her waist while clamping her other hand on the trim around the doorway.

AJ let out a miserable screech of pain and sobbed hysterically. Vicky led the way down, stepping quickly but carefully down the stairs while pulling Katrina after her by the hand. The basement was pitch black save for the tunnel of light emanating from the upstairs hall spilling down the stairs. The girls hit the landing and Vicky slipped her phone from her back pocket, hastily tapping on the flashlight function. A cone of light illuminated the room in front of them, revealing random piles of furniture and boxes. She twisted quickly to the right and screamed.

AJ hung against the back wall of the basement, arms and legs savagely wrapped with nylon rope, digging deep into his skin. His arms were tied to air ducts in the ceiling, lifting him off the ground. His legs were tethered to a water heater in the corner, pulling him to a sharp angle. Blood seeped around the ropes and trickled down his limbs, but it paled compared to the ruin of his chest and stomach. Deep gashes covered his torso, slashing a pattern—a word. With each desperate, but slowing convulsion of breath, blood surged from the wounds. His eyes glazed in the light as he stared hopelessly at the girls. He took one final breath, then his body sagged and his head dropped forward. The sound of blood dripping onto the concrete floor echoed hollowly throughout the basement.

Katrina couldn't scream. She felt her entire body seize up. Her breathing intensified as she hyperventilated. The world turned white, and she felt herself slipping from consciousness. All the while, her eyes were locked on AJ's chest; the image burned into her mind. A single word torn into his skin.

Sinner

CHAPTER 15

Detective Tom Stone sat at his desk in the office. He leaned back in his chair with a mug of stale coffee gripped in his fist, and he took a sip. Beyond his office door, he could hear a jumble of conversation and radio noise. It was a quiet morning at the precinct.

All the days had been fairly quiet since the suicide at Hallberg. Tom was grateful for that. The case had done a number on him. Though they had never found a reasonable suspicion for anything over than a suicide, the whole thing still nagged at him. The parallels with his own daughter's condition were significant, but this wasn't the first case he'd worked on involving a depressed teenage girl, and it most certainly wouldn't be the last. If anything, the world seemed to get more and more depressed as time went on. Tom could feel that in his own soul; some unknown melancholy hanging over his heart like a dark cloud threatening a storm. There was no logical reason for it, but it was there.

He sighed and glanced at the pile of reports on his desk. While most of the current workforce opted to view them on the screen, Tom still liked to print them out. The computer was hard on his eyes. Rifling through stacks of paper made him feel connected to his work. As had been the case for the last several days, there was nothing in the reports to capture his attention. Nothing, at least, interesting enough to pull his mind away from that girl.

He was deep in thought when his desk phone rang. Startled, his hand shook and sloshed coffee onto the arm of his chair. "Damnit," he grumbled. He wiped it away, then rubbed his hand dry on the side of his pant leg and grabbed the phone. "Stone."

"Tom, I got one for you. Come to my office." The line went dead before he could respond, but Tom knew the voice. It was his boss, Chief Maher. He also could tell from his tone that this was not a run-of-the-mill situation. The chief didn't call if it wasn't important.

Tom stood and made his way through the busy precinct. Chief Maher's office door was open, and Tom let himself in without knocking. He found his partner, Elliot Lyons, already seated across the desk from the chief. Chief Bronson Maher was a no-nonsense, intense man. He was a veteran of the armed forces, and his career in law enforcement was rife with accommodations. He was lean and muscular, with an intense gaze befitting someone who had seen so much violence in the world. Rarely had Tom ever seen humor on his face, and he certainly didn't see it now.

"Have a seat, Tom."

Tom nodded and took the empty chair next to Elliot. "What's the scoop?"

"More trouble at Hallberg," Chief Maher replied.

Tom stiffened. "Really?"

"Do you recall interviewing Andrew Beaumont during the Lancaster investigation?"

Tom's stomach rolled. *Fuck me,* he thought, *that little bastard turned me in to his rich daddy.* Tom cleared his throat and quickly composed himself. "I do. He was the kid who hosted the party where the Lancaster girl had been before she killed herself."

"Well, he's dead."

Tom was speechless.

"Dead?" Elliot asked. "What happened?"

"Call came in late last night from campus PD. Two girls went to his house to meet him and found him in the basement, tied up and covered in lacerations. He was alive when they arrived, but died shortly after, according to their statements."

"Another suicide?" Tom asked.

"Doesn't look that way," the chief replied. He opened a folder and slid a photograph across the desk. Elliott leaned forward and retrieved it. He studied the photo for a moment, his face paling, then handed it to Tom.

Tom stared at the photograph and grimaced. The kid was a bloody mess. The skin of his torso had swollen and congealed, but Tom could still make out the word *SINNER* gashed into his chest. "Jesus," Tom said. "He might have been able to carve himself up, but he didn't tie himself up like that. Looks like we've got a murder."

"Looks that way," the chief agreed. "Hard to imagine there's no connection to the Lancaster case. I'm sending you two in to investigate. Let's see if we can wrap it quickly. Whoever did this is deranged. They're going to have a panic on their hands up there if we don't track this person down."

"Understood," Elliot replied. He rose quickly and exited the office.

Tom watched him go, then looked back at Chief Maher.

"Watch him, Tom," the chief said, nodding toward the door. "This one looks nasty. Let's make sure he's up for the task."

"Yes, sir," Tom replied, rising slowly from his chair.

"Are you okay, Tom?" The chief eyed him curiously. "You don't look so well."

"I'm good, boss," Tom said. "Just a little tired. I'll keep the rookie in line."

"Good," Chief Maher replied.

Tom walked out of the office and saw Elliot waiting for him by the front doors of the precinct. He gave his young partner a grim nod, then followed him out onto the street.

Sinner, Tom thought. *Jesus, this is getting ugly.*

They drove the ten minutes of the trip in silence. Elliot Lyons gripped the steering wheel tightly and kept his eyes forward. From his peripheral vision, he could see Tom occasionally glancing his direction, watching him for a few seconds, then turning back. After the fifth or sixth time, Elliot snapped at him.

"What?"

"What?" Tom asked, feigning innocence.

"Why do you keep staring at me?"

"I'm not staring at you. Just checking to make sure you're good. Are you good?"

"Why wouldn't I be good?"

Tom cleared his throat. "Drop the tough guy shit, Lyons. You're new to these kinds of cases, and it can be a lot. The suicide was bad enough, and now this? You and I both know this is related, and if I'm being completely transparent, that scares me. There was some nasty intent with this murder, and someone that would do something like that is likely to do it more than once. This is going to get complicated and heavy, and I want to know if you're good. No bullshit. There's no shame in getting overwhelmed. Ideally, you wouldn't have a case like this so early on, but here we are. It's okay to struggle to come to terms with this and being able to focus and do your job. What's not okay is pretending you're this stone cold professional and then putting you or me at risk if things get heated. Now, I'll ask you again. Are you good?"

Elliot swallowed hard and nodded. Some of the tension eased from his shoulders and he slumped back in the driver's seat. "You're right. I'm sorry I got defensive. It is a lot, but I'm good. Everything you said is true. I'm just eager to get moving and find this guy. I don't want another crime scene like that poor kid."

"Me either," Tom replied. "That kid was an asshole, but nobody deserves that kind of torture."

There was a buzzing sound, and Tom reached into his inside jacket pocket and removed his phone. "Stone, here." After a brief silence, he replied, "understood," and ended the call.

"Chief?" Elliot asked.

"Yes. They've got the two girls who found the kid waiting for us at the health center on campus. Forensics have finished processing the scene. Hopefully, they can come up with something to help."

Elliot nodded. "It can't be a coincidence. I don't want to jump to conclusions, but I think we'll need to bring in the girl's parents. Sinner? That sounds like the psycho-religious stuff they were spewing. If they found out Beaumont hosted the party where their daughter got drunk, maybe they were crazy enough to retaliate? They attacked her roommate, so we know they are capable of violence. This is a whole new level, but they potentially have a motive."

"I agree," Stone said. "Let's find out if they can account for their whereabouts during the murder. I'll have the local PD in their area to pay a visit and see what they have to say for themselves. In the meantime, we'll see what these girls have to say."

They fell back into silence as the miles passed. Forty-five minutes later, the Hallberg Academy bell tower peeked over the horizon. The sight sent a chill down Elliot's spine. It was a beautiful piece of architecture, and it was a shame it would forever be associated with a tragedy in his mind. More than that, though, an uneasiness creeped into his mind as they approached the campus. It had to be the shock of Beaumont's murder, and Elliot knew he had to shake the feeling and focus. He had a job to do. Superstitious was not a word he used to describe himself, but here he was driving toward Hallberg, fighting every instinct in his body to turn the car around and leave.

What's wrong with me? He glanced over at Tom, who stared straight ahead. The man's jaw was set and a tight grimace stretched across his face. *He feels it, too,* Elliot thought. *What are we getting into?*

CHAPTER 16

"Wake the fuck up!"

Paul flipped over onto his back and gazed up in confusion at Dex standing over his bed. Dex grabbed his shoulder and shook him. "Wake up, bro. It's going down."

"What are you talking about?" Paul asked, propping himself onto his elbows.

"AJ is fucking dead, man."

Paul felt as if someone had slapped him. Surely he had misheard Dex.

"Dead. Like murdered. And not just a normal murder. Like some occult ritual fucked up murder."

Paul shook his head. "Slow down. AJ is dead?"

"Jesus, dude, do you not fucking listen?" Dex asked. He paced back and forth around the room. "Fucking wild, Paul. A couple of girls found him at his house strung up in the basement and cut all to hell. Words carved into him and shit."

"Oh, my God. How do you know this?"

"Everybody knows. Campus is crawling with cops. Again." Dex looked at the digital clock on the nightstand by Paul's bed, then rolled his eyes in annoyance. "If you got up before noon, you might know what's happening."

"It's noon?" Paul asked, squinting at the clock. "Wow. I finally got some fucking sleep." There had been no nightmares that night. He had slept through for the first time in weeks. Despite the awful news about AJ, a sense of relief filled him. "When did it happen?"

"Last night. I can't believe this, man. AJ was a good dude. Bit of a prick, sometimes, but he was okay. Why would someone do something like that to him?"

"You said there were words carved on him?" Paul couldn't believe what he was hearing. He was reminded of a scene in The Exorcist where words appeared on Reagan's stomach.

"Well, a word. Sinner."

Paul stiffened and stared at Dex. "Sinner?"

"Yeah, how fucked up is that?"

"Isn't that what the weird girl in our room said to you?"

Dex stopped in his tracks, and his mouth dropped open. "Holy shit, Paul. She fucking did. She asked me if I was a sinner, then told me I was a liar." He returned to pacing the room, more vigorously now, and running both hands through his hair. "What do you think it means? Do you think that weird girl is involved? She wasn't very big. I don't know how she could have overpowered AJ enough to do that to him. I heard he was tied up and lifted off the ground."

"I don't know. But I feel like there has to be some connection. We should probably let the police know. You filed a report about it to the RA, so they can confirm it."

"Yeah, I guess," Dex replied. "This is so fucked."

Paul could only nod. It didn't feel real. He didn't know AJ that well. He'd been to a few of his parties, but they had never interacted outside of those, and none since *that* party. The party Emily came to. The one that changed everything. *Sinner.* The girl in their room. Emily. AJ. They were related, but none of it made any sense at all. His phone chirped, dragging him out of his thoughts. He picked it up from the nightstand and saw a text alert from Tonya.

Call me.

Without looking up, he tapped the call button. After one ring, Tonya picked up.

"Did you hear?" Tonya asked.

"Yeah, just now. My roommate, Dex, told me."

"This can't be a coincidence. It has something to do with Emily. I know it."

Paul sighed. "It might."

"Might? Paul, come on. Did he tell you what was carved into his chest?"

"Yes."

"Sinner? It was Emily's parents. They had to be the ones who did this."

Paul's eyes widened as the sense of it fell into place.

"They must have found out whose house the party was, and they killed him."

"Jesus, Tonya. You might be right."

"I know I'm right. And you know what that means?"

"I...I don't know. What?"

"It means they're going to come after us, too. If they killed AJ for throwing the party, then they're going to come after me for getting her to go. I don't know if they know about you and Emily...being together, but if they find that out, then they definitely will come after you."

"Jesus," Paul breathed.

"We have to go to the police. Like, right now."

Paul looked up to see Dex fixated on him.

"You're right," Paul said. "But there's something else. Dex is coming with us, but we need to talk to you first. We'll meet you in the quad in fifteen minutes, okay?"

"Yeah, see you then," Tonya replied, then ended the call.

Paul sprang out of the bed and pulled clean clothes from his dresser. "Could you hear what she was saying?"

"Not really."

"She's got another theory about who might've killed AJ, and it makes a lot more sense than ours. Emily's parents could've done it. Retaliation for the party where their daughter got drunk."

"Oh, damn. That is good. Those people were unhinged anyway, right? They attacked her roommate."

"Right," Paul said as he pulled a t-shirt over his head and slipped on his shoes. "But I still think there's something to this girl in our room. I think we need to follow both trails and let the cops know. I haven't told Tonya about the girl, and I think she needs to know."

"Why?" Dex asked.

Paul hesitated. He thought back to the night Dex had questioned him about the girl. One thing Dex had said that had never left Paul's mind; *she looked kinda like Emily.* "I don't know," Paul said, "I just do. Just trust me. Let's go."

Dex shrugged his shoulders and followed Paul out of the room. "Whatever you say, man."

Paul led them down the hall and out of the dorm. He wasn't sure if it was the adrenaline of the situation or finally getting a good night's sleep, but he was invigorated. His body rippled with nervous energy, and he pushed the pace as they crossed the street and marched toward the quad.

Tonya saw the boys crossing the quad as she emerged from her dorm. Paul was a few paces ahead and the other guy almost jogged to keep up with him. She waved as they approached and tried to smile, but found she couldn't quite do it.

"Hi," Paul said. His face was flushed, whether from exertion or emotion, Tonya couldn't tell.

"Hey," she replied.

"This is my roommate, Dex," Paul said, waving to the boy beside him.

"Heard a lot about you," Dex replied, sticking out his hand.

Tonya nodded and shook his hand. "Nice to meet you."

"So, listen," Paul started, "we both think you are probably spot on suspecting Emily's parents. But there's something else that happened to Dex that you should know about." Paul looked over at Dex. "Go ahead. Tell her."

Tonya listened as Dex recounted the incident with the strange girl in their room. At first, she didn't understand why Paul wanted her to know about this. At least, not right now with the urgency of their situation. When Dex got to the part about how the girl had asked him if he was a sinner, her opinion changed. She stopped blinking and listened intently as Dex finished the story.

"I reported it to our resident advisor," Dex said, "but nothing else came of it."

"You left part of it out," Paul said. "Tell her what you told me...who she reminded you of."

"Yeah, she looked like Emily."

Tonya closed her eyes. Even before he said it, she knew he was going to say her name. She couldn't escape it. Everything was Emily. It was always Emily. She racked her brain for something logical to say, but every attempt felt hollow and false.

"Do you understand why I wanted you to hear this? Are you thinking what I'm thinking?"

Tonya groaned and shook her head. "I am. I shouldn't be, but I am. A month ago, I would have laughed at you. It couldn't have been her in your room, and it couldn't have been her that killed AJ. I know that." She looked from Paul to Dex, then back to Paul, her eyes glistening. "So why do I believe it?"

Paul sighed. "That's exactly how I feel."

"Wait a minute," Dex said. Understanding bloomed on his face, and he stared at Paul and Tonya with a baffled expression. "You guys think that really was Emily? Like her ghost or something? And her ghost killed AJ?"

"I don't know," Paul said. "Maybe."

"Maybe?" Dex asked incredulously. "Would you listen to yourself? I know you've both been through some shit these last few weeks, but this is too much. That girl's fanatic psycho parents are probably the ones who did this. That girl was weird, but she wasn't a ghost. She was definitely there, real as you or me. I bought in to maybe her having something to do with it because of the sinner thing, but come on, guys. This is nuts."

"That's what I want to think, too," Tonya replied. "I really, really do. But, I've seen her, too."

"Let's stop this and go talk to the cops. If the three of us tapped the parents, I'm sure the cops are already all over that. They've probably already tracked them down and got them in custody. After a gruesome murder like that, they're going to be all hands on deck. We'll go talk to them on the off chance that they haven't already looked into it, and we'll all feel better. Okay?"

"Yeah," Paul answered. "I don't know what to believe anymore, but that's where we need to start. Let's go."

"Thank you," Dex said, clearly relieved. "No wonder you two never sleep. Crazy ass theories like this would keep me awake and loaded down with nightmares, too."

Tonya could only nod and walk along with them. She stayed beside Paul and constantly scanned the quad for anyone suspicious. *Not just for anyone suspicious, but for her.* She held her composure as best she could, but on the inside, she was breaking. For days now, she had constantly felt like she was being watched. Emily's presence was everywhere. She had tried desperately to convince herself that she was imagining everything, but Dex's encounter had cemented her fear.

Emily was still here.

CHAPTER 17

Something was wrong with Vicky.

Katrina kept glancing over at her friend seated beside her in the office. Most of the time, she found Vicky staring blankly at the table, her head drooped and still. But twice, she shifted her eyes over to find Vicky staring at her. Vicky's eyes were bright and twitchy, as if she was boiling over with nervous energy, but the rest of her body was lax and still.

"Vicky, are you okay?"

The campus police had brought them to the health center after the paramedics had checked them over. They had taken a brief statement from Katrina, but told her detectives were on their way to discuss it further. Vicky had not responded to questions from the campus police on the scene. She hadn't spoken a word since they found AJ in the basement. *She's in shock.* That's what the paramedic had said when they examined her. Even in the thirty-five minutes they'd been waiting for the detectives to arrive, Vicky had remained silent and still.

"Please, say something," Katrina begged. "You're scaring me, V."

Vicky turned to face Katrina. Her mouth parted like she was about to speak, but then turned back to the table.

"Fuck, I want to get out of here," Katrina mumbled. She propped her elbows on the table and held her face in her hands. Her phone lay in front of her, and she could see her face reflecting on the glass. Her eyes were puffy and streaks of black mascara trailed down her cheeks. *Ugh, I look like hell,* she thought and leaned forward for a closer look. When she straightened back up, Vicky turned and smiled. Katrina jolted and pushed away from the table. "Jesus, Vicky."

"It's getting better now," Vicky said softly through her smile. Her voice was a wet whisper.

Katrina shrank back further from her friend. "What's getting better? What do you mean?"

"Did you see her?" Her smile brightened, causing her cheeks to dimple. "She was so beautiful."

"Who?"

"She was so pure."

"Who are you talking about, Vicky? Who did you see?"

"She's out there now," Vicky replied, pointing toward the window across the room. "Don't you see her?"

Katrina turned and looked out the window into the lobby area of the health center. She could see the receptionist at the front counter, but otherwise, the lobby was empty.

"The lady at the desk?" Katrina could feel her heartbeat hammering in her chest.

"No, silly. It's her. She came through when we called her, and now she's taking us back with her." Vicky slid her chair away from the table and stood. "She's going to save us. Save us from ourselves."

Katrina watched on in stunned silence as Vicky stepped stiffly around the table toward the window. She crossed from the desk to the window and put her palm on the glass.

"You're right," Vicky said. Her voice was so low and breathy that Katrina barely heard her. She sounded far away, like someone talking in their sleep. "I am a sinner." Vicky reared her head back, arching her neck so that her face tilted toward the ceiling. "Save me." Then, with all her force, she slammed her face forward into the glass.

Katrina shrieked and jumped to her feet, knocking her chair backwards to the ground. There was a sickening snap as Vicky's nose shattered, sending a spray of blood across the window. She reared back again and smashed her face against the glass. The window crunched and spider-web cracks appeared.

Katrina screamed again and looked desperately out into the lobby. The woman at the front desk was standing now. Her hand covered her mouth, and she stared in confused horror at the window. "HELP!" Katrina called.

Vicky thrust forward again. This time, Katrina could hear her tooth smack into the glass. The window cracked further. The woman at the counter looked around the lobby, then shouted for help. Katrina saw her running around the counter toward them from the corner of her eye, but she couldn't take her gaze away from Vicky. Blood splattered the floor and smeared the glass. With a savage grunt, she forced her face into the glass once more and the window shattered. The spray of glass stopped the receptionist just short of the office, freezing her in place. Her eyes were wide with horror.

Vicky reached up and wrapped her hand around a jagged shard of glass still stuck in the frame. She squeezed and wrenched it loose, then turned to face Katrina. Her face was a ruin of blood and lacerated skin. Two of her teeth were missing, and her nose twisted at a sharp angle toward her eye socket. "Forgive us sinners," she said through a mouthful of blood.

Then, with lightning speed, she rammed the shard of glass into her neck. A fountain of blood erupted from the wound, raining across the table.

Katrina screamed and fell back. She bumped the wall behind her and slid to her butt, covering her face with her hands. "No, no, no, no...." Through her own wails, she could hear the receptionist screaming in the lobby.

"Somebody help. Call an ambulance. Call someone. Anyone. PLEASE!"

Katrina shoved her fists in her eyes and screamed in despair. When she dropped her hands and looked out the office door, she saw the receptionist running back to the front desk. She lifted the phone and shouted incoherently at someone on the other end. Then Katrina noticed the figure on the other side of the counter; small and dark, as if made of shadow. Glowing red eyes pierced the darkened face and stared back at Katrina.

It's her, Katrina thought as a wave of dizziness engulfed her, and her vision blurred. She tried to blink through the haze, but everything went white and consciousness left her.

"A unit is on the way, ma'am."

"Please hurry," the receptionist said. She dropped the phone and ran back around the counter. A first aid cabinet hung on the wall across the lobby, and she yanked the door open, spilling boxes of bandaids and ibuprofen to the floor. She scanned the labels and grabbed a handful of the biggest bandages she could find and a roll of gauze. Turning, she ran toward the office. *Why is no one else here?* She made another scan of the empty lobby. Through the open office door, she could see the other girl slumped in the corner and unconscious.

"Please don't be dead," she whispered and forced herself to enter the office and look down at the floor.

The girl lay face down on the tile floor. Dark crimson oozed away from her head and neck in a growing puddle. Her left arm extended, dragging her hand across the pool of blood. The receptionist barely registered the bandages slipping from her fingers and fluttering to the floor. She raised her hands and covered the revulsion plastered on her face. The girl was dead, but in the seconds before she passed, she had written on the white tiles with a blood-soaked finger. There, streaked across the floor like a macabre finger-painting was a word.

SINNER

CHAPTER 18

They could hear the sirens approaching as the health center came into view. Paul and Tonya exchanged nervous glances.

"Now what," Dex muttered.

"We should hurry," Tonya said.

They picked up the pace and made it to the sidewalk across the street just as the ambulance and campus police cruiser screeched to a halt in front of the building. Paramedics scrambled out of the ambulance with triage bags and rushed to the building. The campus security officer ran after them and hurried through the entrance.

"Should we go in?" Dex asked. "Should we wait?"

Before either of them answered, the officer emerged from the building in a panic. His face was stark white, and he clawed at the radio clipped on his shoulder. "We need support right now. We've got a body; a dead girl. Another girl is unconscious. Condition unknown. Jesus Christ, it's a bloodbath in there. Send back up, now!" After releasing the button, he spun around and vomited off the side of the entryway.

Tonya grabbed Paul's arm with both hands and squeezed. She peered up at him with hopeless eyes. "We're too late. It happened again."

"Who is dead?" Dex asked. "Who was in there?"

"I don't know," Paul answered.

"Hey," Dex called out and jogged across the street toward the officer. "What happened in there? Who's dead?"

The officer looked up at Dex and waved him away. "Stay back! This is a crime scene. Stay back!" He spit and wiped his mouth with the back of his hand, then straightened his posture and took a few steps toward Dex. "I can't let anyone in. Move along and stay out of the way."

Dex stopped on the edge of the sidewalk. He looked like he might argue, but then decided against it and walked back to Paul and Tonya. He glanced at the two of them and shook his head. "What do we do?"

"I don't know," Paul replied. His voice was weak and hollow. "I have no idea."

"What?" Tom Stone shouted into the phone.

Elliot jerked his head toward his partner, feeling the nerves in his gut do a somersault.

"Jesus H. Christ," Tom said. "We're en route." He ended the call and dropped the phone in his lap.

"What is it?"

Tom groaned. "We've got another body."

Elliot grimaced and closed his eyes. "Who is it?"

"A witness from the Beaumont murder."

"Holy shit. What happened? Where? I thought they were waiting at the health center?"

"They were. That's where she is. Step on it, kid. We need to get there."

Elliot nodded and pressed harder on the accelerator. Red brick buildings streaked past them and the GPS showed they were only two minutes out. They covered that distance in just over a minute. Elliot braked hard, bringing the car to a stop behind the ambulance. Both men jumped out of the car. Elliot ran around the front and toward the building, but Tom stopped him. He was looking across the street at a group of people on the sidewalk. He recognized two of them. The roommate and the fling; both with ties to Emily's case and now here.

"You three don't go anywhere, you hear me?" Tom called out. "I'm going to want to talk to you."

The roommate nodded vigorously.

"Good," Tom said, then waved Elliot on with him into the building.

The two men crossed the threshold into the health center and made straight for the scrambling paramedics filing in and out of the small office they had used for interviews during the Lancaster case. They could hear a medic calling for a second ambulance. A pale-faced campus officer stood in the lobby with his back to the office. His shoulders heaved up and down and he looked like he had been sick.

"Sir," Elliot called out.

The campus officer looked up at the deceives with a grimace.

"We're detectives Lyons and Stone," Elliot said, flashing an ID.

"Thank God," the officer moaned. "I don't know what to do with this. I'm used to breaking up fights and busting kids drunk in public. This? This is...I can't."

"It's okay, son," Stone replied. "What's your name?"

"Trevor. Trevor Jenkins."

"Okay, Trevor. Fill us in as best you can."

Officer Jenkins took a breath and nodded. "Cindy called it in."

"Who is Cindy?" Elliot asked.

"She's the receptionist they called in today. Normally, the center is closed on Sunday. If a kid is sick on a Sunday or overnight, they have to go to the urgent care uptown. But with what happened, they called her in."

"Got it, go ahead," Elliot urged.

"The two witnesses from the murder were brought here to wait for you guys after we questioned them. Then Cindy called and said the girl was hurting herself. Said she was banging her head on the window and wouldn't stop. That's really all she said. She was in a panic. Dispatch sent us out, and I got here at the same time as the medics. Came inside and found Cindy curled up in the corner over there."

He pointed to the opposite side of the lobby, where a middle-aged woman sat on a cushioned bench with her knees pulled up to her chest. Her eyes were wide, and her body shivered as she stared vacantly across the lobby.

"I went into the office and found the girls. One of them is unconscious, and the other is...deceased. She...uh...she bashed her face to pieces on the window, then severed her throat with one of the broken shards. It's awful."

"Jesus," Elliot whispered.

"Okay," Stone replied. "Thank you, Trevor. Let's take a look, Lyons."

Tom motioned for Elliot to follow him, and they approached the office. The medics were lifting the unconscious girl onto a stretcher. They stepped aside while they wheeled her out.

"Which one is she?" Elliot asked. He pulled a small notebook from his breast pocket and scanned his notes. "Katrina or Vicky?"

"Don't know," the medic answered as they rolled her past. "Didn't check for IDs yet."

They both nodded and let the medics go, then stepped inside the office.

Elliot gasped, and Tom closed his eyes. The smell of blood was heavy in the small room. When he opened them, he let his eyes take in the scene. The girl lay on her stomach, her head turned to the side. A large shard of glass still protruded from her neck, though the blood had congealed and no longer seeped from the wound. Not that there had been much blood left to spill. Nearly the entire floor of the office had become a crimson pool.

"Stone," Elliot said hoarsely. "Look." He raised a finger and pointed toward the girl.

Tom followed his direction and saw it. His muscles clenched and he let out a low groan. "Fuck me."

SINNER

"Did she write that or the other girl?" Elliot asked.

"I don't know. We need to talk to the receptionist. Cindy. At least find out which one is which." Tom turned and walked out of the office with Elliot behind him. "Okay. Let's keep our heads on straight. This thing is moving faster than I'd like, but we have to move with it. We're going to have to divide and conquer here, Lyons. I want you to take the car and go to the hospital. As soon as that girl comes to, we need to find out what she knows. I'll question Cindy and talk to the ones outside. It's not a fucking coincidence they showed up here. No chance."

Elliot nodded. "Agreed."

"Follow up with the captain on your way to the hospital. See if we've got anything on Lancaster's parents. Obviously, this wasn't them, but I still like them for the Beaumont kid. See where we're at and we'll meet back up."

"Yes, sir," Elliot replied and hurried toward the door.

"Lyons," Tom called out after him, stopping the young detective at the door.

"Keep your eyes open. I don't know what's going on yet, but I don't like it. Be ready for anything. And I mean *anything*."

Elliot stared back with a grim expression, then exited the building.

Tom stood still for a moment, trying to collect his thoughts. Outside, he could hear the approach of the second ambulance. He glanced at the receptionist across the lobby, still in a fetal ball on the bench. With a deep sigh, he pulled his notepad from his pocket and crossed the lobby while images of the blood covered office behind him haunted his mind.

CHAPTER 19

"Look," Tonya said.

The doors to the health center opened and paramedics rolled a stretcher out and down the handicap ramp. The girl strapped to it was unmoving, but otherwise did not appear to be injured.

"Who is that?" Paul asked.

They watched nervously as the stretcher wheeled closer to them to be loaded into the ambulance. The paramedics slowed for only an instant while one of them opened the back doors, then they quickly rolled her into the vehicle.

"Oh, shit. I think that was Katrina," Dex said.

"Who's Katrina?" Tonya asked.

"I don't know her very well, but I met her at some of AJ's parties. Pretty wild."

The ambulance fired up its sirens and pulled away from the building. Before it was out of sight, the front door opened again. Detective Lyons jogged down the stone steps toward his car. Tonya waved at him and hurried across the street to meet him at the door.

"Detective Lyons? We need to talk to you."

"Tonya, right? My partner is inside. I have to follow the ambulance to the hospital, but Detective Stone will be out to talk to you. We have questions for you, too. Just stay put out here." He sat down in the car and fired up the engine, then looked up at Tonya. "Stay outside."

"Yes, sir," Tonya replied.

Detective Lyons nodded and closed the door. Tonya stepped away from the car, then returned to the sidewalk while the car sped away after the ambulance.

"What'd he say?" Paul asked.

"He said for us to stay outside and wait for the other detective to come out."

"Okay," Paul said. "I don't love that, but what choice do we have?"

"Why do you say that?" Dex asked.

Tonya answered for him. "The other detective is an asshole. Or at least he was to me."

"Yeah," Paul agreed. "Definitely not as friendly."

"Whatever," Dex replied. "We just need to talk to someone. Do our good deed to help if we can and be done with this mess."

Tonya didn't answer. Her intuition told her they were nowhere close to being done with this. No, she got the terrible feeling that the bad things were just getting started.

Tom snapped his notebook closed and stepped out of the health center. The receptionist had been very little help. The most he had pried from her was the identity of the two girls. Katrina was the one on her way to the hospital. Victoria was the poor girl being prepared for removal from the scene. Her wounds had been self-inflicted. That was all he could confirm. Any sign of her reasoning was currently unknown.

The sun was descending in the west. Tom enjoyed the early sunsets of fall and winter, but right now, he wished for more daylight. Already, the sky was fading into twilight and painting shadows across the landscape. He looked across the street and was relieved to see the three students had listened and stayed put. The girl raised a hand and waved at him.

"Detective Stone," he said as he crossed the street and came to a stop in front of them. "I've met you two," he said, looking at Tonya and Paul, then turned his attention to Dex. "You are?"

"Dex."

"You got a last name, Dex?"

"Yeah, sorry," Dex stammered. "Dexter Lebson. That's my full name."

Tom nodded and scribbled the name on his notepad. "Quite the coincidence to run into you two here. Do you know anything about this?"

"Not exactly," Tonya said. "We were actually coming here to talk to you and your partner about AJ. We were on our way when we heard the sirens."

"I see," Tom said. "Do you have information about Mr. Beaumont's murder?"

"We have a theory," Tonya answered.

"Have you looked into Emily's parents?" Paul asked. "We think maybe they had something to do with it."

"Why is that?"

"Well, they were violent with Tonya, and if they found out somehow that Emily got drunk at AJ's party, they might have wanted revenge. They don't seem to be the most stable people."

Tom eyed Paul appraisingly, then subtly nodded. "We are looking into the Lancasters. We have the local PD in their town working on it as we speak. Not to steal your thunder, but we're on it. Is that all you have?"

"There is something else, but it's a stretch," Paul said.

"Let's hear it," Tom replied.

Paul told him about the girl Dex found in their locked dorm room and how she had asked Dex if he was a sinner. He stiffened at the mention of the word, but didn't let it show. "Did you file a report about this?"

"Yeah," Dex answered. "I reported it to our resident advisor."

"And you had never seen this girl before?"

"No, but she looked...familiar."

"Familiar? Say what you mean, kid. Someone you know, but forget the name, or she just resembled someone."

Dex bounced nervously from one foot to the other and stared at the grass. "She looked kind of like Emily."

Tom stared at Dex with a piercing gaze. "Emily Lancaster? You're telling me this girl you found in your room looked like the girl who killed herself a few weeks ago?"

"Yes, sir," Dex mumbled.

Tom frowned and looked at Paul. "What are you suggesting?"

"I really don't know. I didn't see her, so I can't confirm that she looked like Emily. But it was weird that she asked him if he was a sinner. We heard the word was written on AJ's body, too. That's why we wanted to let you know. It could just be a weird coincidence, but maybe not. We thought this girl might be involved somehow."

Tom slipped his notebook back in his jacket pocket and looked up at the sky. In just the few minutes he'd been outside, it had already darkened further, and the chill was getting stronger. His mind flashed to the crude scrawling of the word SINNER in blood on the tile floor in the office.

"Might be something to it," Tom said finally. "Thank you for letting us know. Young detectives that you are, I assume you've gathered we've got a situation here. Police business, and I won't give details, so I'll need you three to move along. We will be in touch if we have further questions, and you call us if you think of anything else that might be helpful."

"This is all because of what happened, isn't it?" Tonya asked. She looked at Tom with tired desperation in her eyes. "Because of Emily?"

Tom sighed. "I don't know. But we're going to find out. I need to get back inside. You three get out of here. Nothing you need to see."

He watched the three of them turn and slowly walk away from the building. When they were twenty feet away, he called out to them. "Might not be a bad idea to stay together. If this is all related, you kids are involved. Stay together and don't take any chances. I'll be in touch."

They stared back at him ominously. He could see the fear and uneasiness on their faces. They turned and walked away, vanishing into the gloom of dusk. Tom stood silently for a moment, peering up at the sky, then walked slowly back inside the health center.

CHAPTER 20

Elliot checked in with the emergency room desk, then entered the small restroom off the waiting room. He would give the medics time to get the girl to a bed and situated. Katrina Whitmore was her name, confirmed by Tom with the receptionist. He had glimpsed her as they lowered her out of the back of the ambulance and her eyes were open. She wasn't speaking, and she looked disoriented but awake.

Snapping the lock on the restroom door, he gripped the edges of the porcelain sink and dropped his head. The grisly scene in the office stained his mind, and his stomach churned. Elliot turned on the faucet and let the cold water run over his hands. He splashed handfuls onto his face and rubbed his eyes. This was going to be a long night, he knew.

He snatched a paper towel from the dispenser on the wall and rubbed his face dry. When he opened his eyes, something in the mirror caught his attention; on the wall behind him was a red smear. He squinted and turned. The wall was clean. Frowning, he turned back to the mirror and saw nothing unusual. His mind flashed back to the word written in blood on the office floor - the word carved into the chest of AJ Beaumont.

SINNER

Elliot shivered. *Keep it together,* he thought. *Don't let your imagination run away.*

He exited the restroom and returned to the waiting room. Behind the front desk, he could see a paramedic pushing the stretcher back toward the automatic doors. He saw Elliot and nodded back toward the ER.

"She's in her bed now, sir. Number eighteen."

"Thank you," Elliot replied, then looked to the desk nurse. "May I go back?" He showed her his badge.

"Yes, sir," she answered. The nurse reached up and pressed a button. The door to the ER opened, and he stepped through. "Eighteen is all the way back on the left."

"Thank you, ma'am."

Elliot walked through the ER, glancing at the beds as he passed. Only one of them was in use; an elderly man lay sleeping with an oxygen tube trailing from his nose and a heart monitor beeping steadily. A woman sat in the chair by the bed with a bundle of yarn in her lap. Her hands worked effortlessly as she crocheted. Elliot could see the worry on her face. She caught his glance and gave him a tight-lipped smile. He smiled back and moved past.

The curtain was pulled closed in front of bed eighteen, and he gently pulled it open. The girl jumped at his appearance and let out a pitiful yelp. Her eyes bulged, and she pushed herself back against the mattress.

"Oh, I didn't mean to startle you, miss. My name is Elliot Lyons. I'm a detective with the police. My partner and I were on our way to get your statements about what happened with your friend last night. Your name is Katrina Whitmore, correct?"

She stared at him nervously for a moment, then slumped as her tension eased. "Yes, I'm Katrina."

"How are you feeling?"

"I don't know," Katrina replied. "Not good. My head hurts, and I'm really tired. I feel weird."

Elliot nodded and sat down in the chair by her bed. "That's understandable. It looks like you passed out back at the health center. Do you remember what happened while you were there?"

Katrina's face paled. "Vicky is dead, isn't she?"

"I'm afraid so," Elliot answered.

Katrina's lip quivered, and she bit down on it hard. She squeezed her eyes closed but could not stop the tears welling up and seeping through.

"I'm sorry for your loss. I can't imagine how difficult this must be for you, having lost two of your friends in such a short time." Elliot paused. The girl was sobbing now. He stood and pulled three tissues from the box on the counter by the sink and handed them to her. She wadded them up and pressed them to her eyes. Elliot sat and waited silently while she composed herself.

"I'm sorry," she said between gasps.

"Don't be sorry, Katrina. You've been through more than anyone should have to deal with. I wish I didn't have to ask you questions about it all right now, but unfortunately we can't wait. As hard as it must be, I need you to tell me everything you remember from finding AJ last night and what happened at the health center with Vicky. Do you think you can do that?"

Katrina sniffled and wiped her eyes again with the tissues. "Yeah, I think so."

"Okay. Let's start with Vicky. What happened?"

"I don't know. She was acting strange the whole time we were there. She's *been* acting strange, but not like this."

"What do you mean by strange?"

"She wouldn't talk or answer questions. She just stared at nothing, like she was zoned out. Then, just out of nowhere, she started talking like she was answering someone, but no one said anything. It was just me and her in the office. She was saying weird things, and then she got up and went to the window. She banged her face on the window as hard as she could. Over and over. I didn't know what to do. I should have stopped her, but I didn't know how. She was scaring me, and I froze." Katrina broke into another wave of sobs and covered her face with her hands.

"It's okay," Elliot said. "She was being violent, and you could've been hurt if you had gotten close to her. You did nothing wrong."

"That's not how it feels," Katrina said.

"I understand that," Elliot replied. He waited a moment for her to collect herself before continuing. "You said she was talking to someone you couldn't see? Do you remember anything she said specifically?"

"Not really. It's all a blur in my mind. It was a girl. She asked me if I saw her, and something about how she was going to save us. I don't remember anything else. She started...hurting herself right after that."

"That's fine, Katrina. That helps. Let's talk about last night. Walk me through what you remember."

Katrina cleared her throat and wiped her eyes again. "AJ called me and asked me to come over. I asked Vicky to come with me. When we got there, all the lights were off in the house and no one came to the door. We thought he was messing with us. The door wasn't locked, so we went inside. That's when we heard him screaming in the basement. I still thought he was playing a stupid joke on us, but when we got down to the basement and saw him...it was terrible."

"What did you see, Katrina? Take your time and try to remember as much as you can. Anything you remember could help."

"He was tied up on the wall, like lifted off the ground. The ropes were cutting him, they were so tight. He was bleeding everywhere. We didn't know what to do. He was so scared. I've never seen someone so scared."

"Did you see anyone else in the basement with you? Or hear someone upstairs while you were down there?"

"I didn't see anyone, but we wouldn't have heard anything, anyway. He was screaming so loud, and I was screaming. It was-"

Her voice trailed off as the power failed and the emergency room plunged into darkness.

CHAPTER 21

"That's not good," Dex said.

Paul, Tonya, and Dex stopped mid-stride as all the lights on campus blinked out at once. In the distance, there was an audible hum that quickly faded. They had agreed to take Detective Stone's advice and stay together. Tonya made a quick stop at her dorm to pick up some clothes, and they were almost back at the boy's dorm when the power went out. The cloud filled sky stifled any glow from the moon or stars, covering the campus in a thick blanket of darkness.

"No," Paul agreed. "This is not good."

"It's not a coincidence," Tonya stated. "We're past that. She's doing this."

Paul grimaced, but said nothing.

"So, what do we do?" Dex asked. "I don't like the idea of sitting in the dark in our room. We need to do something."

Tonya sighed. "You're right. People are dying. We can't sit around and wait for her to come for the next one of us."

"Listen, guys. I don't disagree that some really weird shit is going down here, but are we really going all-in on the 'Emily is back from the dead and taking revenge' theory?"

"Yes," Tonya replied. She looked at Paul and waited for his confirmation.

"I think we have to," Paul said. "It's straight out of a horror movie, but it's lining up. A month ago, I didn't believe in anything like this. A lot has happened since then."

"Okay, then." Dex replied. "All aboard the crazy train, I guess."

"We need to tell the detectives. Come clean about everything we know...everything we've seen."

"They won't believe us," Dex replied.

"We have to try. They don't know what they're getting into. We have to try." Tonya threw her hands up and waved at the surrounding darkness. "She did this. I don't know how, but she did. She's coming for us."

Paul took her hand and squeezed it reassuringly. "Okay. Let's go back to the health center and see if Detective Stone is still there. If he's not, we'll call him. You've still got his card, right?"

Tonya nodded. "It's in my room."

"Okay. We'll stop on the way and grab the card, then we can call him while we walk. Let's go."

Dex stalled a moment as Paul and Tonya took off back toward the girl's dorm. "This is crazy," he muttered, then followed.

Elliot twisted in the darkness. Somewhere out in the ER, he could hear confused voices. The cease of droning and beeping equipment enveloped the floor in an eerie silence. Elliot retrieved a small penlight from his pocket and clicked it on. The bright white light tunneled through the gloom and illuminated the edge of Katrina's bed. She had scrunched herself into a tight ball. Her mouth was covered with the back of one quivering hand. She stared back at him in terror.

"It's okay," Elliot said. "Just a power outage. They have to have back-up generators here. They'll kick on and everything will be fine, okay?"

Katrina didn't reply. Her entire body tremored.

"I'm going up front to see what's going on."

Katrina whimpered in protest.

"You're going to be fine, Katrina. I'll be right back. The lights will come back on any minute now." He stood and stepped toward the curtain separating the bed from the rest of the emergency floor, then stopped. "Do you have your phone?"

Katrina shook her head. "I...I...don't know where it is."

Elliot shined his light around the room. There was a cabinet on the wall near the bed, and he pulled it open. A purse rested on the shelf inside, and Elliot could see the top of a phone case poking out the opened top. He reached inside and held it up to Katrina. "Is this yours?"

She nodded and reached for the purse.

"Turn on the flashlight on your phone. I'll be right back."

She fumbled with the phone, then the back of it lit up and brightened the room.

Elliot pushed the curtain aside and made his way toward the nurse's station at the front of the emergency room. He kept his flashlight beam pointed ahead, and he could see the shadowy figures of nurses rushing around the desk. As he passed the only other occupied room, he heard the weak voice of the man.

"Ethel, are you there? Why is it dark? I can't breathe very well."

Shit, Elliot thought. *Why aren't the generators on?*

The nurse noticed him approaching. "Sir, I need you to return to your bed. We have a situation here."

"I'm a cop," Elliot replied. "Is there anything I can do to help? Shouldn't the generators have kicked on automatically?"

"They're supposed to, but they didn't. We're trying to get a hold of maintenance to find out why. I don't think there's anything you can do to help right now."

Behind him, he heard the old man call out again. "Ethel! Where are you? Did you leave me here?" His breathing was ragged between his words, and Elliot could hear the panic rising. "Ethel!"

"Is there anything we can do for him?" Elliot asked.

Another nurse emerged from behind the counter. "I'll check on him. Doug isn't answering his radio. Jill, will you please go down to the maintenance room and see if he's there?"

The first nurse nodded and hurried away from the desk. Elliot stepped aside as the second nurse moved past him and stepped into the old man's room. Elliot made his way back to Katrina's room. He could hear the nurse consoling the old man as he passed.

"I'm sure she hasn't gone far, Mr. Windham. She might be in the bathroom."

Elliot frowned. He didn't like the idea of the old woman being stuck in the bathroom in a blackout. Pausing, he pulled aside the curtain and poked his head inside. "Would you like me to go find her? If she's gone to the restroom, it might be dangerous for her to be walking around in the dark."

"Sure," the nurse replied. "Restroom is over on the other side of the nurse's station."

"Got it," Elliot said. He quickened his pace and walked around the central station, shining his light on the opposite wall. The beam hit the restroom sign, and he saw the door was closed. He knocked softly. "Ma'am, are you in there? The power's out. I can escort you back to your husband's room if you need help." He waited a few seconds, but there was no response. Rapping his knuckles on the door again, he spoke louder. "Ma'am, do you need help?"

When she still didn't respond, he slowly pushed the door handle, finding it unlocked. The door swung open and revealed no one inside. Then, from the rear of the emergency room, a scream erupted.

When the power went out, Tom Stone was seized by the strongest gut feeling of his life. His nerve endings fired and muscles flexed. *Something is very wrong here.* Between Tom and the campus officer, they had photographed and secured the scene. The medics had loaded the dead girl onto a stretcher, covered her with a sheet, and wheeled her away. The receptionist had been picked up by her husband and taken home, leaving Tom and Officer Jenkins to lock up the health center until forensics arrived. They were standing at the exit when the lights went out.

"That's odd," Jenkins said. "We don't get power outages here very often except for storms."

Stone grunted in reply. His wide eyes scanned the darkened lobby of the health center. Though he knew everyone else had gone, he couldn't deny the feeling of eyes on him in the darkness.

"I'm going to check with dispatch and see what's going on," Jenkins said. "You need a ride to the hospital?"

Tom nodded. "If you don't mind, yes."

"No problem, sir."

Tom followed him outside and waited anxiously while Jenkins locked the door. The young officer had calmed down considerably after the body had been removed. Tom found him to be very competent at his job. The shock of such a gruesome scene would rattle anyone, but Tom appreciated how quickly the man had recovered.

As they walked to the cruiser, Tom noticed three shapes running across the lawn towards them. Instinctively, he put his hand on the gun holster at his hip and tensed. Then the three figures crossed into the glow of the cruiser's headlights, and Tom saw the panicked faces of Paul, Tonya, and Dex.

"Detective Stone!" Tonya called. "We need to talk to you. Now."

Before he could answer, his phone rang. Tom grimaced and fished in his pocket for it. The surge of uneasiness increased by the second.

"Stone," he said grimly.

"We've got a situation at the hospital," Elliot said. His voice was rushed and his breathing was labored. "Power's out. Generators aren't working. Our witness is hysterical."

"On my way," Stone replied and ended the call. "Jenkins, we gotta get to the hospital ASAP." He turned his attention back to the others. "You three come with us," and motioned to the back of the cruiser.

They loaded into the car, and Jenkins flipped on the lights and sirens.

"Get us there, Jenkins. I've got a bad feeling."

Jenkins didn't question him and romped on the accelerator, pinning them back into their seats, and raced toward the hospital.

CHAPTER 22

Katrina screamed again and covered her face with the blanket. She thought she heard Detective Lyons talking somewhere in the distance, but he wasn't close. Slowly, she lowered the blanket enough to peek over the top. The room was pitch black around her. Only, it hadn't been a moment before.

Red eyes glowing in the dark.

Maybe she had imagined it? After everything she'd been through, who could blame her for figments of imagination? Recovering, she felt around on the bed beside her until her fingers found the phone. She had dropped it when she'd seen the eyes. She picked it up, and the flashlight lit up the space around her bed in harsh brightness. There was no one there.

Footsteps pounded closer, and her curtain jerked aside. Detective Lyons rushed to her. "What happened? Are you okay?"

"I thought I saw something."

"What did you see?"

"I thought someone was in here with me. I saw eyes. Red eyes."

Elliot walked the perimeter of her bed, shining his own light. "There's no one here, Katrina."

She nodded.

"Everything is fine. But we've got an elderly woman wandering around in the dark somewhere. I've got to help find her before she hurts herself. You're completely safe here, Katrina. Just stay put, and I'll be right back. My partner, Detective Stone, is on his way. You've got nothing to worry about."

Katrina could only nod. She quivered, making the blanket twitch against her face.

Detective Lyons patted her reassuringly on the shoulder and then stepped back out of her room. A nurse met him in the hall and he waved her away. "She's okay, just a little worked up. Did you find Ethel?"

Katrina listened to their voices trail away down the hall until silence returned. She took a deep breath and willed herself to stop shaking. *Everything is fine. You've had a terrible day, but everything is going to be okay.*

Somewhere to her left, a soft chuckle sounded.

"Is that what you think, dear? Everything is okay? For a sinner like you?"

Katrina jerked her phone towards the voice and froze.

The old woman stood in the corner of the room, her shoulders hunched and her head cocked to one side, with a gray ponytail hanging loosely, swaying like a pendulum. Her eyes glowed red and a devious grin split her face.

"You like to commune with spirits? With demons? You wear whore clothes and live a life of debauchery. Sin is all over you, sweet one, but you think everything is fine?"

Katrina tried to scream, but it came out in a jagged whimper. Her throat constricted and her breathing became quick bursts.

"An eternity of torment waits for sinners like you. You won't think everything is fine when you swim in the lake of fire with the serpents. No, no, sweet one. You will beg forgiveness, but none shall be granted. Too long you have mocked God. You've thrown your lot with the heathens, and your day of judgment has come. There is no mercy and no salvation."

The old woman laughed and shuffled a step forward.

Katrina shrieked and swung her arms in front of her. Her right hand caught the IV pole beside the bed, sending it crashing to the floor. The old woman chuckled again and shrank back into the darkness. Katrina kicked the blanket off her legs and scrambled to her feet. With her phone gripped in her hand, she leaped over the fallen IV pole and ran for the curtain.

Elliot heard Katrina's scream, followed by the sound of metal clanging. He jerked backward and raced back down the aisle with one hand on his gun and his flashlight in the other; the beam bouncing frantically in front of him. At the end of the hall, he saw the curtain swing open and Katrina staggered into the hall. Like a deer in headlights, she froze in the beam; her face a mask of horror and wide eyes reflecting the glow. Her mouth moved, but no words came out.

"What is it, Katrina? What happened?"

Elliot reached for her, and she collapsed into his arms. The thud of footsteps pounding up the hall behind him, and he glanced back to see the nurse hurrying towards them.

"You're okay, Katrina. What happened?"

Katrina whined; a pitiful moan, and pointed at her room. "She's in there."

"Who's in there?" Elliot asked. He shined his light into the room, but saw only the empty bed, sheets tangled and hanging off the edge. The IV pole lay on the ground. The fluid bag had busted and a small pool of liquid swelled around it.

"The woman," Katrina said. "She's going to hurt me."

Elliot turned and guided Katrina to the nurse. Gently, he pushed her into the nurse's arms. "Can you take her to a different bed?"

The nurse nodded, her face grim and frustrated, and led Katrina back toward the front of the ER. Katrina twisted her arms and turned back to Elliot. "Don't go in there! She's in there!"

"It's okay, Katrina. She's just a confused woman. Her husband is in another room here and she's lost in the dark. She's not going to hurt anyone, and she needs our help."

"No!" Katrina shouted. "You don't understand."

Elliot started to speak, then motion in his peripheral caught his attention. As he turned to his right, he saw a sliver of light reflecting at him from the flashlight beam; a long, skinny, bronze piece of metal arced through the air. In the split second before impact, he glimpsed a liver-spotted, wrinkled hand wrapped around the end.

The knitting needle sank into the soft skin between his throat and collarbone. Pain was instantaneous, both piercing and burning. The shock dropped him to one knee, and he turned toward his attacker. The old woman stood above him leering; a savage look of triumph plastered on her face. Her pupils glowed red like embers in a dying fire. With a grunt, she yanked backward, pulling the needle from him and sending a spray of blood after it. Elliot could vaguely hear screaming, but it sounded far away. The woman drew back again and slammed the needle toward his face. He tried to lift his arm to block it, but the fresh agony erupted from his punctured neck, instead causing him to topple forward into the flow.

The needle pierced through his eye with a sickening sound. Elliot shrieked in tortured pain, and tumbled onto his side. He felt the knitting needle pull loose from the socket, removing part of his eye with it. Blood oozed from his neck wound, and he groaned. He scooted away as best he could, trying to stand, but he could put no weight on his right arm without reigniting the fiery burn in his neck. With his remaining eye, he could see gooey fluid dripping in strands onto the floor from his mangled eye.

With a last desperate push, he got to his knees and lifted with his left arm into a defensive position. Then the needle hammered into his back, dropping him face first to the floor. The needle punctured in and out at a furious pace, but Elliot only felt the first couple. Mercifully, the pain faded, and then he felt nothing at all.

CHAPTER 23

Tom's phone rang, and he answered quickly; the stern voice of the captain on the other end.

"The parent's look clean," he said. "They were at a church function last night with multiple witnesses corroborating their story. Then they hosted dinner at their home for the pastor of their church. We're still checking on a few things, but it doesn't look like they were involved with the Beaumont kid. What's the status there? We get anything from the witness yet?"

"Working on it," Tom replied. "I just finished up with the suicide and en route to the hospital to brief with Elliot. He followed the ambulance to be there when the girl woke up. She was still unconscious when they took her. To make matters even better, there's a campus wide power outage here."

"For fuck's sake," the captain said. "Get there and keep me informed, Stone. This is getting out of hand quickly. I'll make some calls and get you some help. I'm thinking we need more feet on the ground out there."

"Yes, sir," Tom said.

The captain ended the call without another word.

"Step on it, kid," Tom said.

"We're almost there," Trevor replied, but he goosed the accelerator a little harder.

They blew through two more intersections at high speed. Fortunately, traffic was non-existent, and the hospital came into view shortly after. Though the power was out, Tom could still see the large EMERGENCY ROOM sign on the side of the building. Trevor turned hard into the parking lot, tires squealing, then braked even harder under the awning at the drive through entrance. Tom shouldered the door open and stepped out, then turned back and ducked his head inside. "You three stay put."

The kids in the back objected, but he didn't give himself time to hear and slammed the door closed. Trevor was out of the car and at his side, and the two men made for the entrance.

"Sir," Trevor said, then pointed.

Tom looked up and saw the girl, Katrina, from the health center and a nurse running toward the glass doors. The automatic doors were dead, but there was an emergency exit to the side. The door burst open and the two women ran screaming out to them.

"Whoa," Tom called. "What's happening?" Instinctively, he removed his gun from its holster and gripped the handle.

"She killed him!" Katrina screamed.

Tom's stomach turned to icy slush, and his pulse quickened. "Who killed who?"

Katrina collapsed to her knees and sobbed. The nurse looked at him with wild, confused eyes. "The detective that was here. I think he's dead. That woman stabbed him with her knitting needle."

Tom stared back at her as he tried to process what she had said. Then he felt a nudge on his arm. Trevor stepped forward, his own pistol drawn and at his side. "Let's get in there, sir."

Tom clenched his jaw so hard his teeth hurt, then nodded. They walked side by side to the emergency door and stepped through. The ER was a large rectangle with rooms running down each side. The nurse's station desk filled the front center portion, and what Tom assumed to be offices and storage rooms filled out the remaining center of the long space. Both men switched on flashlights. The ER appeared to be empty.

They stood still for a moment, listening for someone moving, but the dark was eerily silent. After a pause, Tom motioned to the right of the nurse's station. "You take the right side, I'll take the left. Stay alert and be ready to act."

Trevor nodded and set off to the right. Tom moved to the left and walked quickly but carefully down the hall. He kept the flashlight beam steady and made sweeping motions to the left and right. Most of the ER room curtains were open, and he scanned them quickly and moved on. When he was halfway down the hall, his light found a dark shape on the floor at the end of the hall. It was a body, and it wasn't moving. The nurse's words flashed in his mind. *The detective that was here. That woman stabbed him with her knitting needle.* For an instant, Tom closed his eyes tightly, praying it wasn't true. Preparing himself for the worst, he pushed forward.

The light found Elliot's face, and Tom groaned. There was no question. He was dead. His right eye was destroyed, and he lay face down in a pool of blood. A wave of nausea racked him, and he doubled forward and closed his eyes. He took slow breaths until it subsided, then called out.

"Trevor, I've got a body."

In the dark, Tom could hear the campus officer's footsteps pounding up the other hall toward the back of the ER. Then they stopped.

"Sir," Trevor called, his voice quivering with uncertainty. "I've got something over here."

Jesus, Mary, and Joseph, Tom thought. *I can't take any more.*

"Sir?"

"I'm coming, kid," Tom shouted back. He couldn't let his eyes linger on Elliot's body. He knew if he looked too long, he'd never let it go. There was a job to do. Now wasn't the time to mourn his partner. He could feel the surge of emotions building in his chest like a tidal wave preparing to smash into the shore and take out everything in its path. It was coming, but he couldn't let it come yet. There was still a job to do. There was no way to get around Elliot's body without stepping into the blood puddle around him. With every ounce of perseverance he could muster, he turned his back to his dead partner and jogged back to and around the nurse's station. As he ran, anger joined the grief stewing in his soul, and he unconsciously tightened his grip on the pistol. His finger curled and tensed around the trigger guard. A blood rage was building; heat emanated from him, turning his face to a crimson red. Whoever did this to Elliot was going to pay.

Taking the opposite corner around the station, he flinched and stopped, jerking his pistol hand up into a firing position with the flashlight braced underneath it like a scope. Something had moved past him in the dark. He had seen the dark shape scuttle by him in his peripheral; no features, only a shapeless mass moving away through the dark. He scanned the front of the ER in steady, quick strokes with the light, but saw no one in the area.

"Detective Stone, sir," Trevor called from behind him. "I need you back here."

Tom noticed the steel confidence the young officer had developed since they left the health center had wavered in his voice. He took one more sweep of the entryway with the light, then turned back and hurried down the hall. Trevor came into view near the end. He stood staring into one of the ER bedrooms. As Tom approached, Trevor did not turn to him, but simply pointed toward the bed.

Inside the room, an elderly couple lay on the bed. The man wore a hospital gown, the front of which was covered in a blossom of blood. His gown was torn open on the chest, and Tom could see ragged flesh where something had stabbed into him. The woman lay curled up beside him. A bronze knitting needle was shoved deep into her nostril. Only a few inches of the metal rod extended from her nose; enough for a small fist to grip.

They were both dead.

Tom and Trevor stood beside each other; neither moving, neither speaking. Tom had witnessed all manner of violent crimes in his career with the police force, but never had he been exposed to this much violence, murder, and suicide in such a short time. He suddenly felt very old and very tired. After a long moment, he finally retrieved his phone and called dispatch.

"Detective Stone onsite at Hallberg University. Officer down. Multiple casualties. I need assistance."

Tonya slapped at the window of the police cruiser. On the other side, Dex tried in vain to shoulder the other door open.

"You're gonna hurt yourself, man," Paul said. "It's a cop car. The back doors are always locked."

"Let us out," Tonya shouted as she continued to slap the glass.

The nurse finally turned and looked at the cruiser. She looked confused and unsure of what to do. She spoke to the girl clinging to her side and nodded toward the car. The other girl stared at Tonya with dazed incoherence and shrugged her shoulders.

"That's Katrina," Dex said. "She's okay."

Tonya increased the force and speed of her blows on the window until her hands ached. Finally, the nurse walked to the cruiser, opened the front passenger door, and leaned inside. "Are you three under arrest?"

"No, we're here to help," Paul said. "The cops brought us with them."

"Please, let us out," Tonya begged. "Bad things are happening, and we can't be stuck in this car."

"And we know her," Dex added, pointing toward Katrina. "That's Katrina. We go to school with her."

The nurse nodded, seemingly convinced by their urgency and Dex knowing the girl's name. She leaned back out of the front seat and opened the back door. They scrambled out of the cruiser and created a huddle on the sidewalk, minus Katrina, who stood shakily a few feet away from the group.

"What happened in there?" Tonya asked.

The nurse crossed her arms and shook her head. Her face was pale and grim. She started to speak, then stopped, a look of confusion creasing her brow. "Did you hear that?"

"Hear what?" Paul asked.

The nurse didn't answer. She cocked her head and looked at the darkened alcove of benches to the side of the emergency room entrance.

Then, her voice taking on a monotone drawl as if she were hypnotized, she said, "but I'm a nurse. I help people every day. I'm not a sinner."

Katrina yelped and spun toward the nurse.

"Oh, shit," Dex said.

Suddenly, the nurse lurched into motion, walking briskly toward the alcove of benches. "Don't be silly. Let me help you."

"No," Tonya shouted. "Stop!"

The nurse did not react to Tonya's warning and faded into the dark corner. She stopped and leaned forward, then her body stiffened and her head snapped back.

"Not good," Dex whispered. "This is not good."

Still with her back to the group, the nurse laughed. "The work of the hand of God is never done. Sinners are everywhere. There are four right behind me now. A witch who converses with demons; a glutton who spoils his soul with an excess of debauchery; a manipulator enticing the good with the ways of the wicked; a corrupter, seizing and seducing the innocent. All crimes against God. I am the wrath of God; judge, jury, and executioner. I find you all guilty, and vengeance is mine to reap." She slowly turned and faced them, her eyes glowing red in the dark. "The punishment for sin is death."

Katrina let out a piercing scream that split the night.

"Go," Dex shouted. He shoved Paul and Tonya with both hands, then ran to Katrina and wrapped his arm around her. "Split up and don't stop. Run!"

Katrina did not have to be told twice. She gripped Dex's hand in hers and ran, dragging him behind her. Paul took Tonya's hand, and they sprinted away from the cruiser in the other direction, back toward campus. Behind him, he heard the nurse bellow a howl of rage and charge after them.

CHAPTER 24

Tom and Trevor burst through the emergency door and out into the night. The back passenger side door of the cruiser was open and all three kids, plus Katrina and the nurse, were gone. In the distance, Tom made out shapes running away.

"Over there," Trevor said, pointing in the opposite direction.

Tom looked that way and saw more shapes running.

"Fuck me," Tom said, then turned to Trevor. "Take your cruiser and go get them," he said, nodding to the runners Trevor saw first. "I'll go after the others on foot."

"No, you won't," Trevor said, and tossed Tom the keys to the car. "With all due respect, sir, I'm in better shape to chase someone on foot. You take the car."

Tom gritted his teeth and almost fired back, then realized the young officer was right. His running days were pretty well behind him. "You're alright, officer," he replied. "Go."

Trevor nodded, then took off in a blur of speed. Tom didn't waste time watching him go and rushed to the cruiser. He fired up the engine, hit the sirens, and floored it. The exit lane out of the emergency room parking lot forced him to take his eyes off the runners for a few seconds, but as he peeled out onto the road, he thought he glimpsed shadows vanishing behind a building in the distance. He grunted in frustration and pressed harder on the gas. Brick buildings blurred past him. When he reached the intersection near the building where he'd last seen them, he braked hard and took the corner, with squealing tires clinging desperately to the pavement.

"Fuck!" Tom roared at the dash. He flipped on the brights and slowed the cruiser. The campus was eerily devoid of pedestrians, which helped his cause, but he saw no sign of the runners. He cursed again and creeped forward while scanning the surrounding buildings for any sign of movement. Something must have caused them to run. His mind flashed back to the gruesome scenes in the emergency room, swapping between Elliot's savaged body and the grim display of the old couple. All sense of reason was lost, and Tom was out of his element. Whatever was happening on this campus was unnatural. There wouldn't be anyone to arrest for these crimes, and Tom didn't know what to do with that knowledge. What was the endgame? He didn't know, but what else was there to do but keep going? With grim determination, he kept searching.

Dex heard Katrina gasp and then her hand slipped from his grip. He spun and saw her thump heavily onto the grass. She moaned in pain and wrapped her arms around her stomach.

"Shit, are you okay?" Dex asked, dropping to one knee beside her. His eyes darted back and forth between her and the yards and buildings behind them. "Can you get up?"

"Yeah," she hissed between lurching breaths. "Is she…coming?"

Dex shook his head. "I don't see anyone, but we can't stay here. We have to get somewhere safe."

Katrina pushed herself onto her hands and knees and stood shakily. "Is anywhere safe?"

Dex wanted to say yes, but he knew it was a lie. Instead, he put his arm around Katrina's shoulders and helped her along. He knew she couldn't keep the same pace with him, so he let her lead.

"Where should we go?" Katrina asked.

"I think away from people," Dex replied. *If this thing can possess people, then we should try to keep our distance.*

"I don't think it matters," Katrina said. She sounded defeated and hopeless. "It can make you do things to yourself, too. That's what happened to Vicky. It made her kill herself."

Dex winced. "I will not let anything happen to you, okay? We're going to stay together and figure this out."

Katrina smiled weakly and leaned into his shoulder. "I guess we'll find out. I hope you are my hero."

Me too, Dex thought to himself. *Me too.*

"Hey! Hold it, right there!"

Dex froze, and Katrina jerked herself against him. They turned and saw the glow of a flashlight bouncing toward them.

"Officer Trevor, Hallberg PD."

"He could be lying," Katrina whispered.

Dex nodded and pulled her tighter.

The officer stopped ten feet from them and kept his flashlight aimed at their faces. Dex could hear the man panting to catch his breath. "Why did you run from the hospital?"

"The nurse. She came after us," Katrina said.

"The nurse attacked you?"

"Yeah," Dex replied. "After you guys went inside, she freaked out and came at us. We split up and ran. I think she followed Paul and Tonya."

The officer was silent for a moment, then his flashlight eased to the ground. "Jesus, what is going on around here? Detective Stone was in pursuit of them. If she attacked you, then she could have been responsible for the others in the hospital. We need to get you two somewhere safe. Do either of you live on campus?"

"I do," Dex answered.

"Which dorm?"

"Lynwood."

The officer nodded. "Okay, that's close. Let's get you to your dorm, then I'll rendezvous with Detective Stone."

Dex didn't have a better alternative, so he tugged Katrina with him and they followed the officer. A five-minute walk later, they reached the rear entrance of Lynwood Hall. The card reader device by the door was out with the rest of the power, but the officer unlocked the door manually with a campus master key. He ushered them into the hall and stood in the doorway.

"Get to your room and stay there. Lock the door and don't open it for anyone except the police. Do you understand?"

Dex and Katrina nodded in unison.

"Good. I'll be back when we get this buttoned up." He closed the door and took off, leaving them standing in the entryway. Behind them in the lobby, a group of students were playing cards by candlelight.

Katrina eyed them warily, then looked at Dex. "Away from people," she whispered.

Dex took her hand and led her to the stairwell. A minute later, they were in Dex and Paul's room. Dex closed and locked the door, then pulled his computer chair over and wedged it beneath the handle. As satisfied as he could be, given the situation, he went to Katrina. She stood in the middle of the room with her arms wrapped around her chest. He tried to think of something to say that would calm her, but he had nothing. Instead, he leaned in and hugged her tight. She clung to him and cried.

Tonya felt like they'd been running forever. Her lungs burned, and a throbbing pain swelled in her side. Despite the ache and exhaustion, she forced herself to keep going and match Paul's pace. Sweat glistened on his forehead, but his breathing was steady, and he did not appear to be struggling as much as her. Tonya couldn't hear the nurse behind them anymore, but hadn't dared to slow down and look back.

Paul must have noticed her struggle to keep up with him, and veered off their current path, pulling her with him behind a large oak tree and pausing. He positioned her with her back to the tree, then leaned out and looked back the way they'd come. Tonya studied his face for any sign of alarm.

After a moment, he nodded. "I think we lost her. I don't see anyone."

Tonya scanned their surroundings. The buildings on campus all carried the same aesthetic, but with the power outage, everything had become a red brick mirage that seemed the same no matter where she looked. She had lost all sense of direction and had no clue where on campus they currently were. "Do you know where we are?"

Paul looked around them thoughtfully. "This has to be north quad," he said. "Unless we accidentally doubled back, we ran too far to still be on the south side."

Tonya considered and then looked in the direction they had been running. In the distance, she could vaguely make out the looming shape of the bell tower. "You're right," she said. "Look, there's the tower."

"Okay, yeah," Paul said. He studied for a moment, then shook his head in frustration. "Well, now that we know where we are, do we know where we're going? Tonya, I don't know what to do. Where can we go so that she won't find us?"

"Nowhere," Tonya replied. "There's nowhere to hide. She'll find us wherever we go. And now we know she can take over people. Nowhere and no one is safe. We can't hide, and we can't run. We have to fight."

"How?" Paul asked. His voice was desperate and defeated. "How can we fight this?"

Tonya's eyes found the shape of the tower again; a black silhouette against the night. "I don't know yet, but I think we have to go there." She pointed a steady hand at the tower. "That's where this started. Maybe that's where it has to end?" It was a question, but she didn't mean it to be. Something inside her pulled her toward the tower. That was the place Emily had taken her own life, and if this was going to end, somehow she knew it had to end there.

Paul looked at the tower. "I guess I don't have any better ideas. This has to end, one way or another."

Tonya held his gaze for a moment, his words lingering in her mind. *One way or another.*

Tom cursed and slapped the steering wheel again. He had driven circles around campus, but he'd lost all trace of the runners. Hell, he wasn't even sure which kids he was looking for. He pulled the car to the curb and parked for a moment, then grabbed his cell phone and called Trevor. He listened to silence as the phone tried to connect. When it didn't, he looked at the screen and saw SOS where the signal bars should be.

"God Damnit!" In a fit of rage, he threw the phone onto the floorboard of the passenger seat. With a defeated groan, he threw the cruiser back into drive and sped back onto the road. Campus buildings blurred past him as he raced down the street. He knew he was being reckless, but if he didn't find them soon, he feared what he would find later. He didn't know if he could stand to find another body.

As he banked hard into an intersection, he glimpsed a figure staggering off the sidewalk and into the street. He sucked in a lungful of breath and slammed the brakes, but he was going too fast. At the last second, he recognized the pale green scrub pants and top of the nurse from the hospital. Their eyes met for a split second; her gaze was menacing, and she sneered at him as her body slammed into the front of the cruiser. Tom cried out as she flipped onto the hood and her face collided with the windshield. There was a crunching of glass and red spray coated the web of cracks. The car lurched to a halt, and Tom heard her body thump forward and roll back onto the street.

"Jesus Christ," Tom gasped, then scrambled out of the car. The smell of radiator fluid assaulted his senses and steam hissed from the crumpled hood. He ran to the front and found the nurse laying on her back. Blood poured from her broken nose, and she coughed and gagged as it streamed into her mouth and down her throat. He dropped to his knees beside her and tried to roll her onto her side, but she screamed in agony, setting off a coughing fit that sprayed blood all over Tom's face and arms. She looked up at him, and Tom realized something had changed. The eyes that stared at him now were scared and desperate. There was no longer any sign of the malice and wickedness he had seen for the split second before impact.

She tried to speak, but it came out as a garbled choke and another spray of blood. Tom reached for his pocket to call for an ambulance, then croaked in frustration as his hand hit the empty pocket. His phone was on the floorboard of the car. He pushed himself up and made to run for the car, then froze.

A black figure stood beside the cruiser. He might not have seen it at all were it not for the glowing red eyes. His blood ran cold, and he felt rooted in place. The black figure began to shimmer and come into focus. When it stopped, he gasped.

"I tried to kill myself because of you, Dad."

"No," Tom moaned. This wasn't possible. She couldn't be here.

"You weren't there when I needed you. What other choice did I have? Who can you turn to if not your father?"

"No, baby, you're not here." Tom felt his eyes burn with tears. This thing in the road looked like his daughter, sounded like his daughter, but it couldn't be. "You're not here."

"I'm not here," the spectre agreed. "I'm at home, in a tub of red water, wishing you would've stopped me."

"NO!" Tom screamed. "YOU ARE NOT REAL!"

The image of his daughter shimmered and dissipated, leaving Tom sobbing in the street. He covered his face with his hands and screamed with all his might; a violent roar that echoed off the buildings nearby. When he regained control of himself, he let his hands fall. The nurse lay dead at his feet, eyes vacant and staring at the sky.

CHAPTER 25

Paul stared up at the bell tower. He'd never really paid much attention to it during his time at Hallberg University before Emily. It was impressive and aesthetically pleasing, but quickly faded into the background of the campus scenery. Now, it towered above him like a monument of doom casting long shadows over everything around it.

He felt Tonya slide her hand into his and squeeze.

"Now what?" He asked.

"I think we need to go up," Tonya replied.

Paul turned to her. "Do we have to?" He knew the answer already, but couldn't stop himself from saying the words. Every instinct in his body told him to run. Keep running. Run forever if you have to, just don't go up the tower.

"I think we do. It feels right. I can't explain it, but it does."

Paul swallowed the lump in his throat. Before he could change his mind, he strode to the door on the backside of the tower. The door was painted and fashioned to look like the walls of the tower, and in the dark it was easy to miss, but he found it quickly. Tonya watched nervously for any sign of the nurse or anyone else while he turned the knob.

The door was locked. Paul tried again, but the knob wouldn't turn. He tried pushing his shoulder into the door and turning, hoping the latch would pop, but it held fast.

"Well, shit," Paul muttered.

Tonya groaned.

"It makes sense. After what Emily did, I'm sure they make sure this door is locked all the time."

"There has to be another way in," Tonya replied. "I know this is what we have to do."

Paul stepped back a few steps and peered up at the sheer face of the wall. Like all the buildings, most of the tower was constructed of red brick, none of which allowed much room for hand or footholds. "We're definitely not climbing it."

Suddenly, there was an audible click. Paul looked at Tonya, feeling his color drain. There was no mistaking that sound. To confirm it, he stepped forward and slowly turned the knob. It rotated easily, and the door creaked open.

"She wants us to come up," Tonya said.

As if in answer, a steady breeze swept through, picking up swirls of dry leaves and twisting them in the air.

"If this is what she wants, do you still think it's a good idea?" Paul asked.

"It's the only idea I have left," Tonya said. She took his hand once more and pulled him toward the open door. Her mouth was set in a determined line. "We have to end this."

Paul wanted to say something to change her mind. Anything that would take them away from this place. Instead, he only nodded, and let himself be led into the darkened stairwell inside the tower.

They climbed the stairs silently. The door creaked closed behind them, shutting out the last remnants of light. They moved cautiously but steadily, one flight after another. After six or seven flights, Paul felt his thighs and calves burn with exertion. He let go of Tonya's hand and gripped the railing for support.

"You okay?" Paul asked. He could just see Tonya's figure moving a few stairs ahead of him in the dark.

"Yeah," she replied breathlessly. "I'm just out of shape. If we get through this, I'm never running again."

Paul chuckled. "I don't mind running, but I'd like my life not to depend on it." Making the joke seemed to lighten the mood enough to make him forget what they were doing, if only for an instant.

"I think we're almost to the top," Tonya said.

Paul heard her pick up the pace and jog up the next few stairs.

"Hey, be careful," he called out. "I can't see shit in here."

Above him, he heard a door creak, and a glow of moonlight filtered into the stairwell. He gritted his teeth and pushed himself up onto the last landing. He could see the open doorway at the top of the tower, and Tonya had already stepped out onto the balcony.

He reached for the railing, but hissed in surprise as a bone white hand reached out of the darkness behind him and clamped around his wrist. He choked out a gasp and twisted back. The dark figure of Emily stood behind him. Her dark hair hung in dank clumps around a chalk-white face, emphasizing the crimson glow of her red eyes radiating from within.

"Do you want to go back to your room, Paul?"

Trevor had jogged a few blocks from Dex's dormitory when he spotted the bicycle. He rushed over to it and nearly pumped his fist in triumph to find it not chained up. He needed to move faster. Detective Stone could be anywhere, and Trevor needed to back him up. He made a mental note of the building and a promise to return the bike, then pedaled off toward campus. *Never thought I would have to commandeer a bicycle*, he thought and laughed out loud. It was all he could do to keep his wits about him, given the circumstances of the night. This is why he'd gone into the police force to begin with. He wanted to help people. It didn't matter the situation. He was trained to act in any crisis, and this certainly fit the bill, however bizarre it became.

Trevor pedaled hard and raced through the streets and sidewalks of the campus, searching for any sign of his cruiser or Detective Stone. He cut between buildings and through the quad areas, but saw no one save for a few students loitering around their halls. At last, he pedaled out of the south quad and onto Chestnut Street, and found what he was looking for.

His cruiser was parked a half mile up the road with the lights still flashing. Trevor could see Detective Stone standing in the street near the cruiser and there appeared to be someone else on the ground. Trevor doubled his pace, standing up on the pedals and pushing the bike as fast as he could get it to go. When he reached the cruiser, he squeezed the hand brakes and kicked the bike sideways.

"Jesus," Trevor said as he took in the sight of the battered nurse on the street. The detective turned a dazed expression on him. Trevor could see the man had been crying. He looked at the cruiser and saw the shattered and bloodied windshield. "Detective, are you okay? What happened?"

Detective Stone lifted his hands and waved at the car, then at the nurse, then at nothing. He mumbled something incoherent and shook his head. *Fuck me,* Trevor thought. *He can't give out on me now.*

"Did you hit her?" Trevor asked, motioning toward the nurse.

"She hit me," the detective finally answered. "Ran out in front of me. Couldn't stop."

Trevor nodded. "I understand. Did you find the other kids?"

Detective Stone shook his head.

"It was an accident, sir. I know you're upset, but it wasn't your fault."

Stone looked at him in confusion.

"The nurse? I can see you're upset because you hit her."

"She's dead," Stone moaned.

"I know, sir, but like I said, it was an accident."

"Not her," Stone shouted. "My daughter. She's dead!"

Trevor's brow crinkled. "Sir?"

"My daughter is dead. She killed herself."

"How...how do you know that, sir?"

"She told me."

"Who told you?"

"She did! My daughter was here, and she told me."

Trevor nodded. He thought he understood what was happening. The detective must have hit his head in the accident. Or he was in shock. "Sir, I'm sure your daughter is fine. Your daughter isn't here. She's back at home, right?"

Stone stared back at him. His eyes were wild and weary at the same time. "What?"

"Your daughter isn't here, sir. She's at home. She doesn't go to this school. She couldn't have been here. I think maybe you have a concussion?"

Stone pressed his hands to his head. Trevor could hear him taking deep breaths. After a moment, Stone looked up at him. "Maybe you're right. She's not here. Couldn't be here."

Trevor nodded encouragingly. "That's right, sir." He approached Stone and gently put an arm around the detective's shoulder. "Let's get you in the car and call this in. Get you checked out and go from there."

"Okay," Stone answered, and let Trevor lead him around to the passenger door of the cruiser. "Yeah, that's what we should do."

Trevor pulled open the passenger door, but before Stone had time to sit down, a scream split the night. Both men jerked upright and looked toward the sound. The bell tower stood in the distance, and Trevor glimpsed movement at the top.

Stone saw it too and pointed. "Up there! They're on the tower."

"Get in," Trevor said as he sprinted around the cruiser and jumped in the driver's seat. The car was still running and engine lights glittered on the dashboard. The temperature gauge hovered perilously near the red end of the gauge, and he noticed the heavy scent of antifreeze. He held his breath and put the car in reverse. The one working headlight cast its glow on the body of the nurse, causing him to wince. He hated to leave her there, but what choice did they have? There would be a lot of explaining to do when this is all over, and that would just have to be another one of the things. Praying the car would make it to the tower, he backed it onto the curb, then sped up toward the tower.

Tonya edged toward the railing of the tower balcony. At this height, the wind was ferocious and bitingly cold. The ground below seemed impossibly far away. A shiver ran through her, and her teeth chattered. She wrapped her arms around herself and tried to shake off the cold, nervousness, and fear forcing her body to shake. She glanced back at the open door, but Paul had not yet emerged onto the balcony. He had been right behind her, and his absence made her uneasy.

"Paul?"

There was no answer from inside the stairwell.

Feeling a panic surge in her chest, she hurried back across the balcony to the doorway. "Paul!"

Paul stepped into view on the landing just as she hit the opening. She stopped herself with both hands on the frame. "Jesus, Paul. You scared me."

Paul stood still in the shadows of the stairwell, with his head cocked to one side and his body twitching sporadically.

"What are you doing?" Tonya asked.

Paul's voice came from the shadows. "I scared you? Why would you be afraid? What have you done to warrant such fear?"

Tonya gasped in dawning horror. *No. Please no.*

"What guilt riddles your conscience that gives you reason to fear me? Would you confess to your sins? Would you face your judgment with bravery and accept the consequences you are due? Or will you keep running from your guilt to an inevitable end?" Paul stepped forward, letting the moonlight spill onto his face. His blue eyes turned crimson and streaks of blood trailed down his cheeks. "Are you a sinner, Tonya?"

Tonya couldn't bite back the terror any longer and a guttural scream ripped from her throat. She stumbled backwards, never taking her eyes off Paul, but painfully aware of the railing approaching behind her. The stairwell foundation blocked off three quarters of the balcony, leaving her nowhere to go except back...back against the railing. "Paul, please. Fight her. You can fight her."

Paul snarled. "This one is the most vile of sinners. His punishment will be extraordinary, and his will is broken. Defiling the innocent to curate his lust. A heathen of the most foul."

Tonya sobbed in protest. "Emily, please! I know it's you in there. Paul didn't mean to hurt you. I didn't mean to hurt you. We are both so sorry for what happened, but neither of us are bad people. We're not sinners."

"Lies upon lies," Paul hissed. His blood filled eyes glowed as if a flame had been ignited in his sockets. "You enticed and corrupted goodness to grow the army of the damned. This one was all too eager to deflower me in my compromised state. A state that you encouraged."

"I'm sorry," Tonya cried. "I'll never forgive myself for what happened, but you have to know I meant no harm. And you were a good person, Emily. Things happened you regret, but you didn't have to do what you did. This all went too far."

Paul roared in anger. "How dare you cast your blame on me! You and your kind soiled me beyond salvation, and yet you dare to deny your guilt. Oh, the fires of hell will erupt with your arrival." Paul took a few more jerking steps toward her.

Tonya reflexively stepped back and felt the cold metal railing press into her back. "Please fight her, Paul. Please."

"Your time of judgment has come, Tonya. The angels weep, but vengeance shows no favor." Paul strode quickly forward and swiped at Tonya. His hand smacked the side of her face and knocked her back hard into the railing.

"Get down!"

Tonya flinched at the sound of the voice. Her eyes jerked to the stairwell behind Paul, and she saw Detective Stone standing in the doorway. His gun was drawn and aimed at Paul.

"DROP!"

Paul hissed and spun around. Tonya closed her eyes and dropped to her knees.

The shot sounded like a cannon blast. The bullet hit Paul in the chest. He spun with the impact, staggered, then dropped to one knee. Tonya watched on in despair as the campus police officer emerged from the stairwell. He rushed past the detective and shoved Paul onto the ground. Paul groaned in agony, but bucked against the young officer. In a flurry of movement that seemed impossible, Paul was back on his feet, dragging the officer with him. With inhuman force, he grabbed the officer by his shoulders and drove him headfirst into the iron railing. Tonya screamed as the sound of his neck breaking pierced through the wind.

"NO!" Detective Stone raised his gun and fired again. This time, the bullet split the back of Paul's head open in a spray of tissue and gore, and he collapsed onto the body of the officer. Neither of them moved again.

Tonya covered her face with cold hands and screamed with every ounce of energy she could muster.

Paul was dead.

Tom barely registered the gun slipping from his fingers and clattering to the concrete floor of the tower balcony. He couldn't take his eyes off the bodies. The kid was dead. The shot to the chest should have incapacitated him, if not killed him, but somehow it had not. Because of that, Trevor was dead, too. Trevor was dead. The kid was dead. Elliot back at the emergency room. The nurse in the street. The girl at the health center. The Beaumont kid. All dead. Every corner of Tom's mind was filled with images of the dead. The girl's screams blended with the howling shriek of the wind, forming a symphony of horror scoring the most tragic of stage plays. He might have stood there in that lost daze forever, but then the girl stopped screaming, and he saw why.

A dark swirl of shadows slithered from the pile of bodies in front of them, twisting and undulating until it was an upright figure; stark white skin with strings of matted black hair. The figure stared at the girl with eyes of roaring flame.

Tom shook his head, trying to wrap his brain around the impossible things unfolding before him. He saw the girl slowly stand and face the apparition. There was a desperate intensity on her face, and she squared herself. "This ends now, Emily. Once and for all."

A voice, barely a whisper, floated on the wind, emanating from the figure. "Will you answer now for your sins?"

The girl roared in hopeless frustration. A battle cry into the night. Then she gritted her teeth and stared defiantly. "I am not a sinner, and if I am to be judged, then so will you."

Before Tom could realize what was happening, the girl sprinted forward toward the figure with a savage scream. She collided with the apparition, and to Tom's astonishment, it held form and buckled against her. The girl clamped her arms around the thing and powered her legs forward, driving them both across the balcony and into the railing. With a final scream, she thrust her hips forward, lifting them both up and over the railing.

"No!" Tom shouted. He dove for the railing and reached for the girl's foot, but he was far too slow and she dropped out of sight. An instant later, Tom collided with the railing and peered down at the ground below. His despair broke through in torrents of wails and tears. The girl's body lay on the sidewalk below. He saw no trace of the black figure.

Tom stood atop the bell tower alone, surrounded by death.

EPILOGUE

"**H**ey, are you awake?"

She opened her eyes and blinked them into focus. Dexter smiled at her. Katrina stood next to him. Her face was weary and tired, but she managed a small smile of her own.

"Hi, Tonya," Katrina said. "How are you feeling?"

"Like I fell off a bell tower," Tonya replied. Her voice was a hoarse croak, and she had to strain to make any sound at all. She was in a full body cast and completely immobile. Fluid IVs and feeding tubes snaked from her ports to the stands by her bed. It had been two weeks since her fall. Everyone agreed it was a genuine miracle she had survived. She had broken her right leg, multiple ribs, her collarbone, fractured six vertebrae, and suffered a severe concussion. It defied all sense of physics; an unbroken fall from that height should have killed her. Yet, she was alive. She had undergone four different surgeries to insert plates and screws into various bones. The surgeons were optimistic that in time, and with extensive physical therapy, it was absolutely possible that she would walk again.

You are one lucky young woman. That's what the doctors kept telling her. She thought about her dead friends and wondered if that was really true. Tonya cleared her throat and looked at Dex. "Have you seen her?"

"No, still no sign of her," Dex replied, his smile fading. "I think she's gone, Tonya. I really do."

Katrina nodded. "I'm not having nightmares anymore, either."

Tonya sighed. "I haven't either. I'm just afraid to let my guard down. Not that I could do anything about it if she showed up now."

"I don't think she will," Dex said. "If you ask me, I think you put her to rest."

Tonya smirked, but didn't respond. She hoped he was right. It was a miracle she survived the fall, but not in the sense the doctor's thought. Despite her concussion, she vividly remembered the fall. It couldn't have taken more than two seconds to hit the ground, but time had ground to a halt while she plummeted to the ground. She had held tight to Emily's ghastly form the whole way down, never breaking eye contact. In that last instant, the red glow had faded and for a fraction of a time, she looked like herself again. A wave of emotion had overcome Tonya. There had been a glimmer of sympathy and regret on Emily's face. At the last second, before impact, Emily had rolled them over and hit the ground first, acting as a cushion for Tonya. Her fading ethereal form had not been enough to save Tonya from injury, but it had been enough to save her life. In the days following the surgery, she had confided all this to Dexter and Katrina. She desperately wanted to believe it was over now; that her brazen act of sacrifice had awoken an understanding in Emily's tortured soul, and now they could both rest.

Katrina reached out and gingerly took Tonya's fingers and entwined them with her own. "I'm so sorry, Tonya. None of this would've happened if we hadn't call for her. I'll never forgive myself."

Tonya squeezed Katrina's fingers as best we could. "We talked about this, Katrina. I blame myself just as much as you blame yourself." Katrina had told Tonya on one of the first visits to the hospital about the seance she had performed with Vicky and AJ. After everything that had happened, Tonya's world views differed from what they had been before, and she didn't question the truth of her story. They had mistakenly allowed Emily to come back, full of rage and hate. At first, she was ashamed to admit she had been angry with Katrina. It was easy to put blame on her for all the tragedy that followed. But she realized how hypocritical it was for her to let her own guilt in Emily's suicide lead her to latch on to blaming someone else. "You have to find a way to let it go. We all have to. We were lucky enough to make it through this, so we have to honor this second chance we've been given."

Dex put his arm around Katrina and pulled her to his chest. She let herself be comforted. Tonya was happy for them. She didn't really know either of them very well, but it made her happy to know they had each other. It reminded her of the fleeting moments of comfort she had shared with Paul. There was power in sharing a burden with someone else who understood what they were carrying. Her sadness was that the person who stood with her was now gone. In this way, she envied them, but not so much that it denied her support.

"She's right, Kat," Dex said. "We've all been through some horrible shit, and we made mistakes, but there's nothing we can do to change that now. All we can do now is learn from our experiences and be better people than we were before."

"Fuck off, Tony Robbins," Katrina said with a chuckle. She looked up and gave Dex a kiss on the cheek.

"I'm just a bottle of fucking sunshine. You're gonna have to learn to live with that," Dex said.

"I could probably use some more sunshine in life," Katrina said. "I'm pale as fuck."

"I like it. My vampire lover."

"Get out of here," Tonya said. Their banter made her feel good, but she could already feel the next round of pain meds hitting her system and bringing the wall of sleep with it. "If you guys make me laugh or puke, it's gonna hurt like hell."

"Okay, okay," Dex said. "Get your rest, Tonya. We're gonna be okay."

Tonya nodded. She couldn't bring herself to say it. Not yet, anyway. She just hoped.

"Oh," Dex said, stopping short as they walked to the door. "Detective Tom was leaving when we were coming in. We ran into him in the parking lot. He came to check on you, but you were asleep. He said he's retiring. They put him on administrative leave or something pending the investigation, but he's not going back. Said he wants to spend more time with his family."

"I don't blame him," Tonya said. "This would be enough for me to quit law enforcement, too."

Dex chuckled. "No shit. He's a good guy, though. I thought he was a dick at the beginning, but he's alright."

Tonya's mind filled with the image of Detective Stone shooting Paul on the bell tower. She knew she could never scrub that picture from her memory, but she also knew the man had saved her life. "Yeah. He's alright."

"Take it easy, Tonya. We'll be back to see you in a day or two."

Tonya smiled, wiggled her fingers in as much of a wave as she could manage, and watched them go. The steady beep of medical equipment joined with the dizzying effects of her pain meds pulled her to the edge of sleep. *Please, let this be over,* she thought, and let herself drift away.

Henry Lancaster held the wooden matchstick with trembling fingers and touched the flame to the candle wick. It caught and pale light bounced on his weathered face. His wife, Janet, sat silently at his side.

"Be at peace, brother."

Henry looked up at the man across the table. His name was Hezekiah Watson. He was a burly man with a finely trimmed beard, dressed in black slacks and a button-up shirt.

"You've nothing to fear," he said. "Your desire for vengeance is your God given right. Did not Jesus raise Lazarus from the dead?"

"Amen," Janet hissed.

"Did our lord God not destroy Sodom and Gomorrah for their trespasses?"

"Praise him," Janet cried. Her face flushed with anger and spittle coated her lips.

"Brother Henry, cast your doubts aside and embrace the will of God."

Henry nodded and leaned back in his chair. This all felt surreal to him. The corruption of their daughter had tortured them. Days and weeks had passed, but the anger and desire for justice would not falter. Henry had confessed this to their pastor multiple times. The last of those conversations culminated in Pastor John's referral to Hezekiah Watson.

"The rage you feel is fueled by injustice done to you and yours by the Devil himself," Pastor John had said. "It is in times like these, we must ask God to grant us his vengeance."

Henry had not known how to respond. Never would he have imagined Pastor John would recommend this; a seance to call on their lost daughter and ask God to make her his ethereal hand of wrath. It felt wicked. They were crossing a line Henry had always considered uncrossable, lest his soul be lost. To call to the dead? What sort of witchcraft or black magic would do such a thing? And would it not leave a stain on their very souls? Henry had said as much to Janet, but she would have none of his concern. Even more so than he, Janet brimmed with fury. Henry had never seen such hatred, and it scared him. He was as devout as he could be in his faith, and his soul was broken from the shame his daughter had brought them. Still, this seemed a step too far.

"I see in your eyes that you still doubt, brother Henry," Hezekiah said. "For God to hear us, we must be strong in our faith."

"I will be strong enough for us both," Janet said. She glanced spitefully at her husband. "If you are too weak to seek justice for this travesty, then go away. I will put things right."

"No," Henry said, feeling heat rise in his cheeks. "There will be no need for that." He turned his attention back to Hezekiah. "Do what you must so that God may grant us the redemption we seek."

Hezekiah nodded solemnly, then lowered his head and hummed; a droning, monotonous sound that reminded Henry of a swarm of bees. Janet took his hand and squeezed fiercely.

"I call to the land of the dead in the name of God the almighty. Bring forth Emily, so that she may speak for her sins and let God's wrath flow through her." Hezekiah returned to humming and swayed in his seat. "I am an instrument of the Lord and speak in His name. I demand you come forth, Emily. Come forth and stand for your sins."

Henry's eyes were closed, but he felt the change in the room. The hairs on his arms stood and his skin rippled with goosebumps. The air was electric, so much so that he could hear a dull crackling sound. Beside him, Janet let out a gasp and then a victorious cry, and he opened his eyes.

Next to the table, between him and Hezekiah, stood a vision of Emily. She looked as she had the day they dropped her off at the university, pure and innocent. She gazed around the room with a look of confusion. Her eyes found her parents, and a sob escaped Henry.

"Emily, my dear," he said.

Emily spoke, her voice echoing and faint. "What have you done, father?"

Hezekiah spoke for him. "We have called you from the dead by the will of our God to wreak vengeance on those who tainted you and drove you to sin."

"Yes!" Janet shouted, raising her hands in triumph. "Bring the wrath of God to them all!"

Emily's gaze drifted from Hezekiah to her mother, and then to her father. "My sins are forgiven," she said.

"Praise God for that," Hezekiah said. "Now, you must accept this gift from Him, and bring destruction to those who brought you to this fate."

Henry flinched as Emily's appearance changed. The glow of her skin faded. The volume of her hair dissipated until her dark locks lay in matted tangles around her now pale face. Her voice came in a deeper pitch, guttural and thick.

"So it shall be. I will have my vengeance."

"AMEN!" Janet shouted.

Emily lurched forward and clamped a milk white hand around her mother's throat. She jerked Janet to her feet and held her bewildered face inches from her own. "For the false mother, who shamed a child for the mildest of discretions, who taught hate and bigotry instead of love and compassion." She forced Janet's head down until her face hovered above the flaming candle. The fire licked at her eyes and her eyebrows curled and burned away. Janet shrieked in pain and struggled to free herself, but Emily's grip was unbreakable.

Henry and Hezekiah both jumped to their feet. Henry staggered backward, covering his mouth in ghastly horror. Hezekiah turned and ran for the door. Emily snapped her free hand in his direction, and the door slammed closed. He yanked desperately at the handle, but it would not budge.

The smell of burning flesh and hair filled the small room. Janet's hair ignited, and still Emily held her down. The candle flame grew into a roaring blaze, catching the tablecloth and the table ablaze with unnatural speed. Janet choked out another anguished scream, then slumped forward onto the burning table and stopped moving.

The fire spread quickly, as if the room had been doused with gasoline. Hezekiah shouted and banged on the door, but help was not coming. Henry shrank back into the corner of the room and stared at his daughter. The fire danced all around her, but didn't touch her. She sauntered toward him, pinning him to the wall.

"I'm sorry, Emily."

"It is not for me to forgive you," Emily said. "As you've wished, I am not salvation. I am vengeance."

Flames engulfed the room. Henry heard Hezekiah screaming as the fire consumed him. He could feel his own skin burning, but he couldn't look away from his daughter.

"It's time now, father. Come with me," Emily said. Her eyes glowed red like rubies embedded in white rock. "Hell awaits."

ACKNOWLEDGEMENTS

Many thanks go out to my usual crew of supporters. This book was the first time I've written a story inspired directly from a cover. Matt Wildasin posted this cover as a pre-made for sale, and I fell in love with it. This story doesn't exist without that inspiration. Thank you, Don Tackett, for editing this thing into shape and seeing all the things I couldn't see. Thank you to Chuck Buda for being a constant support and never letting me wander too far off the tracks.

And as always, thank you, reader. If you took a chance on this story, I am grateful, and I hope you enjoyed the ride. Please take a minute and leave a star rating or review on whatever platform you bought the book. It really makes a difference.

Until next time!

ABOUT THE AUTHOR

Steve L Clark is an author of horror and dark fiction from Southwest Ohio where he lives with his wife and children. For book news, blog posts, links to social media, and to buy signed paperbacks, visit stevecl arkbooks.com

www.ingramcontent.com/pod-product-compliance
Lightning Source LLC
Chambersburg PA
CBHW061350310726
48974CB00001B/280